THE HARMONY SIX

AND THE LEGACY OF
IRON MAN OF INDIA

VIDYA SAGAR
VEDANABHATLA

To my beloved family, whose love and support light every path I walk.

*To my wife, **Swapna** — my rock, my muse — whose strength and grace inspire each page.*

*To my daughter, **Siya** — my spark of joy — whose curiosity and spirit breathe life into every corner of this tale.*

*And to my son, **Vishwa** — my joy and future — hoping these tales of heroes inspire the greatness within you.*

*This book is for you, my heart's home. **Always.***

<u>**Disclaimer:**</u> "This Book is a work of Fiction based on real-life characters"

Contents

Foreword

Somewhere along the way, we forgot.

We forgot the soul of our stories—the heartbeat of our past.

We forgot that history was not merely myth.

It was memory.

The India we pass down to our children today is often filtered through foreign eyes, flattened into dates and dynasties, or dismissed as distant legend.

What gets left out?

The spirit. The depth. The dharma. The resilience.

The truth.

That is why I wrote *The Harmony Six*—and why I will keep telling more stories, through this series and beyond it.

Not as fantasy. Not as fiction.

But as a call to remember.

A Story Meant to Be Told Together

I don't just want you to read these stories.

I hope you will tell them—to your children, your parents, your friends.

I hope a child carries *The Harmony Six* to the dinner table.

I hope a mother remembers something her grandmother once whispered—and tells it anew.

Because when stories live in families—not just in books—they grow roots that no storm can tear away.

These books are meant to be shared.
Spoken aloud.
Questioned.
Carried forward across generations.

Come, Sit By the Fire

Let's journey together—into memory, myth, and meaning.

Let's raise children who aren't just proud of where they come from, but who understand it—and carry it forward with strength and tenderness.

The future belongs to those who remember where they came from and choose to carry that wisdom with grace.

Chapter 1

Whispers of a New Beginning

"Ammaaa!" Siya's voice pierced the early morning silence.

The clock read 5:30 AM. Siya was wide awake, her heart already drumming. She tried to fall back asleep, but the buzzing anticipation refused to quieten.

Siya sat up, blinking as the dim glow of streetlights filtered through the curtains. She paused before pulling open her curtain. Something about the morning felt different. Like the air was holding its breath. Like something… was waiting.

Her eyes flickered to the world map on her bedroom wall—tiny flags marking every city she wanted to visit. Her mind raced with thoughts of school and the exciting news awaiting her.

Siya loved her school: the classes, the teachers, and especially her friends. But today, her enthusiasm was at a new high.

"*Amma, wake up!*" she called out again, just as the clock cuckooed six times, gently rousing her mother from sleep.

Her mother stirred, her voice tinged with mild surprise and concern. "*Did I miss my alarm? It's not 6:30 yet, is it?*" she mumbled, her mind racing through the morning routine ahead of the school bus's arrival.

"*No, it's not 6:30, but I just couldn't wait any longer! Today is important at school!*"

Siya's mother pulled the blanket over her head. "*Important day, or just your usual over-excitement?*"

"*Amma, I'm serious! Ms. Shehnaz said there's going to be something big today. I can feel it!*"

Her mother sighed, amused. "*Did she actually tell you that, or is this your overactive imagination?*"

"*No, Amma, she did say it—well, almost. She mentioned it's something 'exciting and meaningful' for students like me.*"

"*Students like you?*" her mother asked, raising an eyebrow.

"*You know—kids who love history and geography.*" She twirled dramatically. "*And discovering new things!*"

"*Or students who enjoy waking up the entire house before sunrise?*" her mother teased, pulling a pillow over her head.

Siya huffed. "*Nanna's already awake!*"

"*Because Nanna is already cooking for you two little rascals,*" her mother muttered, rolling onto her side.

Realizing she wasn't going to win this battle, Siya bounced off the bed.

"Fine! But I will blame you if I miss the most important day ever!"

Stepping into the hallway, Siya was greeted by the rich aroma of sizzling dosa batter.

She grinned as her dad flipped dosas like a champ in the kitchen. In the background, a pressure cooker whistled away, likely filled with tomato pappu (dal) or potato curry for lunch.

"Good morning, Nanna!" Siya greeted, snatching up a steel tumbler of warm milk from the counter.

Her dad, still in shorts and a T-shirt, flashed a smile over his shoulder. *"Good morning. You're up early."*

"Not early enough!" Siya said between sips. *"Amma thinks I'm making too much fuss about school today!"*

Her father chuckled. *"You do tend to get super excited about school pretty often..."*

"Nanna!" Siya pouted.

"Just saying," he teased, flipping another dosa onto a plate. *"Eat first. Worry about changing the world later."*

Siya plopped down at the table, feeling like something was off.

"Wait—where's your lazy son?" she asked, raising an eyebrow.

Her father sighed. *"Vishwa's still snoozing. Better wake him up, or I'll have to do it my way."*

Siya grinned. Everyone knew that when Dad said, "my way," it meant turning off the fan and yanking off the blanket—a fate way worse than Mom's morning nagging.

She dashed to Vishwa's room and pushed the door open.

Sure enough, he was buried under his blanket, sprawled out like a starfish. Next to him, an open comic book teetered on the edge of the bed.

"Vishwaaa! Wake up!" Siya shouted, shaking his shoulder.

Vishwa, who was in second grade at the same school, wasn't a morning person. He was pretty sure that grown-ups had invented mornings just to ruin everyone's fun.

"Mmmph… five more minutes…" he mumbled, as usual.

Siya smirked. *"Oh well, guess I'll just have your dosa then."*

Vishwa's eyes flew open. *"You wouldn't dare!"*

"Oh, I definitely would," Siya said with a grin, turning to leave.

Vishwa shot up so quickly he almost toppled off the bed. *"I'm up, I'm up!"*

Vishwa, still half-asleep but managing, sat at the dining table and dug into his dosa. Their father packed their school lunches: chapati, dal, potato curry and a tiny packet of potato chips.

"Siya, how many dosas did you eat?" their dad asked, *scooping more batter onto the pan.*

"Just two."

"Liar. I saw you sneak a piece from Vishwa's plate."

"That doesn't count," Siya said with a mock-innocent smile.

"It absolutely does," Vishwa muttered through a mouthful of dosa.

Their mother walked into the kitchen, her cotton saree neatly draped, her wet hair tied into a low bun.

"Siya, got everything? Books? Water bottle?"

"Yes, Amma!" Siya said as she grabbed her bag and adjusted the small globe keychain on the zipper.

"What about you, Vishwa?" their mother asked.

Vishwa stretched and said, *"I've got my books, my lunch, and... my cricket ball."*

Siya facepalmed. *"This is school, not the IPL, Vishwa."*

"You never know," Vishwa shrugged.

By 7:10 AM, they were already at the front gate of their apartment complex, waiting at the school bus stop.

Most days, they barely made it on time, but today they had a few extra minutes to spare.

"Why are we so early?" Vishwa yawned as he leaned against the gate.

"Because for once, I didn't have to drag you out of bed," Siya replied smugly.

The school bus rumbled to a stop, its yellow doors creaking open, and Siya climbed in first, quickly scanning the familiar rows of seats.

Just as expected, Dharani and Ajay were already inside, sitting opposite each other.

Ajay was hunched over his notebook, scribbling furiously, his left foot tapping the floor, deep in concentration. Meanwhile, Dharani sat by the window with a half-finished sketch in her lap, completely lost in thought.

"Copying homework again, Ajay?" Siya teased, sliding into the seat next to Dharani.

Twelve-year-old Ajay, two years older than Dharani and in the same class because he repeated a grade, grinned sheepishly. Once Siya's classmate, Ajay found some subjects challenging. Despite his academic struggles, he was well-liked for his easy-going nature and knack for making friends laugh.

Ajay didn't even look up. *"It's called last-minute revision."*

Dharani smirked. *"Right, like you totally knew about the test before this morning."*

"Of course I did," Ajay said, flipping the page dramatically. *"I just… forgot to study and finish the notes."*

Siya rolled her eyes. *"Keep this up, and one day you'll forget so much you'll end up in my brother's class."*

"Hey!" Ajay shot her a mock glare. *"I'd make an awesome second grader."*

Dharani giggled, tucking a strand of hair behind her ear. *"But would second graders even want you?"*

"Wow. Betrayed by my own friends." Ajay exclaimed, clutching his chest as if wounded.

Siya laughed, then turned to Dharani. *"What are you sketching today?"*

Dharani looked down at her lap, where the faint outline of a bird in mid-flight was taking shape.

"I'm trying to draw a koel, but I can't seem to get the wings right," she admitted, chewing on the tip of her pencil.

"It looks fine to me," Siya said.

"Yeah, well, you think every bird is a crow unless it's a peacock," Dharani teased.

Siya gasped. *"That's not true!"*

Ajay grinned. *"Name five birds that start with the letter 'K'."*

Siya opened her mouth, then quickly shut it.

"That's what I thought," Ajay said with a smirk.

Dharani chuckled and nudged Siya. "It's okay, you're good at history. I'll handle the birds."

Siya sighed dramatically. *"Fine, but when we go on a real adventure, I'm leading."*

Ajay gave her a skeptical look. *"Are we going on an adventure?"*

"Not yet," Siya quickly said. *"But one day."*

Dharani smiled. *"Just make sure you don't mistake a pigeon for an eagle when that happens."*

Siya groaned while Ajay and Dharani burst into laughter.

As the bus approached the next stop, Vishwa eagerly peered out the window. The bus doors opened, and in hopped Subhas and Sarojini, the 7-year-old twins and Vishwa's best friends at school.

Subhas, always the dreamer, had wild tufts of hair sticking up at odd angles, as if he'd just run straight out of a storybook. Sarojini, ever the planner, wore her hair neatly combed and pinned back with two tiny clips. Their uniforms were a little faded, and their shoes looked polished one too many times.

"Sarojini, over here!" Vishwa called out excitedly, patting the seat next to him. *"Saved this spot just for you!"*

The twins, bright-eyed and bubbling with energy, quickly settled in, boosting the lively atmosphere even further.

Sarojini beamed and took the seat next to him. She placed her small, slightly worn lunch bag on her lap, just as Vishwa pulled a neatly wrapped extra chapati roll with potato curry from his bag and handed it to her.

"I asked Amma to pack an extra one for you today," he mentioned casually.

Sarojini blinked, looking at the roll. *"Vishwa, you really didn't have to—"*

"I know," Vishwa grinned.

Sarojini smiled, accepting it without another word. That was how their friendship worked—no questions, no need to explain.

"Hey, hey, hey!" Subhas leaned in, grinning. *"What about mine?"*

Vishwa rolled his eyes. *"Only if you beat me at rock-paper-scissors."*

"Challenge accepted!"

The two boys launched into an intense battle, while Sarojini placed the food into her lunch bag quietly, a grateful glimmer in her eyes.

Siya turned back to Dharani and Ajay.

"Okay, now that everyone's here, let's guess what the announcement might be."

Dharani tapped her pencil against her chin. *"Maybe a school competition?"*

Ajay shook his head. *"Too basic."*

"How about a science fair?" Sarojini suggested.

Ajay made a face. *"Ugh. Science fairs are just volcano models and boring chemical reactions."*

Siya smirked. *"I thought you loved science."*

"I love sci-fi!" Ajay exclaimed. *"Think robots, space travel, parallel dimensions. School science? Just a bunch of already known facts."*

"So, you only like science if it's made up?" Dharani asked, amused.

"Exactly!" Ajay grinned.

"You are going to fail your physics exam so badly," Siya muttered.

Ajay shrugged. *"Maybe, but if aliens invade tomorrow, I'll be the only one prepared."*

Dharani rolled her eyes. *"Yes, Ajay, because aliens are definitely going to come to Bangalore first."*

"You never know."

The bus rolled toward school, morning sunlight streaming through the windows. Siya glanced outside, her excitement bubbling up again.

They had no idea what the announcement would be, but something told Siya —

It was going to change everything.

Chapter 2

The Announcement

The school bus rolled into Harmony Public School, joining a stream of yellow buses unloading eager students. Children rushed inside—adjusting ties, slinging backpacks, chasing friends, all heading for the assembly hall.

Siya stepped off the bus and took in the familiar sights: the neem tree by the gate, the school dog napping near the bicycle stand, and the tall glass windows of the library—her favourite place—reflecting the golden morning light.

"Come on, Siya, let's go!" Dharani urged, nudging her forward.

They headed towards the large assembly hall, where students in neatly pressed blue and white uniforms were already filling the rows, their chatter echoing off the high ceilings. Teachers guided younger students and silenced whispers with practiced glares. Near the stage, the principal and vice principal were deep in quiet conversation.

Siya and Dharani snagged a spot near the front. Vishwa and Subhas were already whispering in the boys' line. A few rows behind, Sarojini chatted quietly with other girls.

"What do you think the announcement will be?" Dharani whispered.

"A new art competition, maybe?" Dharani grinned. *"I nearly won last time. This time, first place is mine!"*

"You and your paints," Siya smirked. *"I'm hoping for something adventurous. A field trip to a historic place would be amazing!"*

Ajay, standing a few rows behind Vishwa, caught Siya's eye and winked, giving a thumbs-up. Later, when they talked, he'd probably say, *"Unless it's a computer lab or a cricket pitch, count me out."*

The air buzzed with anticipation. Even the teachers seemed unusually alert.

Suddenly, the microphone crackled. A hush fell over the assembly when Ms. Shehnaz, their history teacher, took the stage. Her smile carried a hint of mystery, and her eyes twinkled like stars. She paused dramatically, relishing the thick anticipation in the air.

"Good morning, students!" Her voice echoed through the hall, capturing everyone's attention. *"Today,"* she began, leaning forward slightly, *"I have something truly*

extraordinary to share with you." She paused again, allowing the excitement to build even further.

"*But first, let me ask you this: how many of you have ever dreamed of stepping into history—not reading it, but living it?*"

A wave of murmurs swept through the hall—some students exchanged curious glances, while others simply waited. Siya's heart pounded like a drum; she could barely breathe. This was it—the announcement she had been waiting for!

Ms. Shehnaz continued, "*Well, now's your chance. Because our school has been chosen... for something special.*" There was a slight pause. "*A journey to one of the most powerful symbols of our nation—the Statue of Unity in Gujarat!*"

For a brief second, silence fell—as if the entire hall needed a moment to digest the news. Then, the room burst into cheers, with students leaping to their feet, clapping, and whooping.

"*Did she just say the Statue of Unity?*" Dharani gasped.

"*The statue of Sardar Patel?*" Siya exclaimed, her eyes lighting up.

Vishwa's face lit up with the prospect of exploring a new place. Ajay sighed, already bored, and shifted from foot to foot like he'd rather be anywhere else.

"All this build-up... and it's just a history trip?" he muttered under his breath, shaking his head.

Ms. Shehnaz held up a hand, motioning for silence. The hall gradually quieted, though the energy remained electric.

"But," she continued, *"this trip is more than mere sightseeing. It's a journey into history. We will explore not only the life of Sardar Vallabhbhai Patel but also the values that shaped our nation: unity, leadership, and courage."*

Siya beamed with excitement. This was exactly the kind of adventure she had hoped for!

"The school will partially sponsor this trip," Ms. Shehnaz added, *"but each student will need to contribute ₹1000 for the three-day journey. Those interested should talk to their parents and submit their payments within the next few days."*

The excited buzz in the hall dimmed slightly.

Murmurs spread through the hall as the cost was mentioned. Siya and her friends exchanged excited glances, their imaginations already running wild with the adventures ahead. However, for Subhas and Sarojini, the excitement quickly faded.

Their smiles slipped away, replaced by a silence only they understood.

The twins knew their parents—migrants from West Bengal who worked tirelessly as support staff at a nearby hospital—struggled to make ends meet. Managing school fees was already a challenge; how could they afford ₹1000 for a trip?

It wasn't even a question.

Just moments ago, the trip had seemed like a reachable dream—a chance to explore, learn, and be part of something big.

Now, the dream had already begun to fade.

Chapter 3

....

The Cost of a Dream

The assembly hall doors burst open, spilling students into the courtyard, buzzing with excitement.

"I can't wait!" Dharani gushed. *"I've already planned what to pack—my sketchbook, colours, and—"*

"Snacks?" Ajay chimed in with a smirk.

"For you—obviously," Dharani shot back, grinning.

All around them, students excitedly discussed the trip—where to sit on the bus, which teachers were coming, and what they'd do in Gujarat.

Siya felt the same rush of excitement, but something caught her attention.

A short distance ahead, Subhas and Sarojini walked side by side—silent, unlike the chattering others.

They walked with their heads bowed, the spark gone from their steps, replaced by a quiet heaviness.

Sarojini clutched her school bag tightly, as though she held something much more fragile than books. Beside her, Subhas kicked a small stone along the pavement, his expression unusually serious.

A sinking feeling settled in Siya's stomach. Something was wrong.

Then, it all clicked.

Of course.

She'd noticed the signs before—second-hand books, folded lunches, the way their parents politely declined events that cost extra.

₹1000 per person was just too much.

Siya's excitement faded. A moment ago, it had felt like an adventure. Now, it just felt unfair.

She knew she had to do something.

Siya turned away from her friends and walked straight to Ms. Shehnaz.

"Ms. Shehnaz," she began, her voice steady but firm. *"I want to help."*

The teacher, who had been flipping through some papers, looked up. *"Help with what, Siya?"*

"It's Subhas and Sarojini," Siya said. *"I think they can't afford the trip—and I want to help. I'd like to pay for them with the money I won in various competitions this year."*

Ms. Shehnaz's gaze flickered with surprise.

"That's incredibly generous of you, Siya," she said, her tone warm yet measured. *"But are you sure? That money is yours—earned from your hard work."*

Siya hesitated for a brief second.

That money came from months of studying, rehearsing speeches, and burning the midnight oil. It was hers. But they needed it more.

But then she thought of Subhas and Sarojini.

She remembered their quiet disappointment.

They hadn't complained. They'd simply accepted it—quietly.

Siya nodded firmly. *"I'm sure, and I know my parents won't mind either."*

Ms. Shehnaz studied her for a long moment before smiling.

"Alright," she said gently. *"I'll speak with your parents first. If they agree, we'll make this happen."*

Siya nodded, her chin held high, a determined glint shining in her eyes. Helping others was just who she was. This time was no different.

Her parents would support her—she was sure of it.

As she walked back to her friends, a new spring in her step, she felt a purpose in her step. She'd made a difference—and she knew it.

A few steps away, Subhas and Sarojini walked silently side by side, their minds burdened with heavy thoughts.

Little did they know, a friend was already paving the way for them to join this exciting journey.

That afternoon, Siya sat across from her father at the dining table, nervously twirling the edge of her dress while explaining everything.

Her father listened in silence; his expression thoughtful.

He repeated slowly," *So, you want to use your savings to help your friends?"*

Siya nodded, determined.

For a moment, he said nothing. Then, his face softened.

"I'm proud of you, kanna," he said, gently squeezing her hand. *"Helping a friend is always worthwhile. Remember, good deeds always find their way back to us."*

Siya released a breath she hadn't realized she was holding.

Later that evening, Ms. Shehnaz spoke with Siya's parents, who readily agreed and even asked if there was more they could do to help.

The next day, Ms. Shehnaz discreetly called the twins' parents to assure them that the school would cover the entire cost of the trip. She wanted to honour Siya's wish to keep her contribution anonymous. When Subhas and Sarojini heard the news, their faces lit up with joy.

"What? We're actually going?" Sarojini whispered, her voice trembling with emotion.

Their mother nodded, eyes shining. *"Yes children. Everything's taken care of."*

Subhas and Sarojini threw their arms around their parents, overwhelmed by their emotions.

"We're going! We're actually going!" Sarojini exclaimed, laughing through her tears. Their minds buzzed with excitement. That night, sleep barely touched them.

The days leading up to the trip were a whirlwind of activity. The rustling of backpacks, the vibrant array of clothes and travel guides, and a palpable anticipation in the air enveloped the children in a joyous storm of preparation.

Armed with her extensive knowledge of geography and history, Siya became an impromptu guide for her friends. She had read several books and articles about Sardar Vallabhbhai Patel, the "Iron Man of India," and the history of Gujarat. She had even watched documentaries about the construction of the Statue of Unity, the world's tallest statue. As they packed their bags, she shared fascinating facts and stories, her enthusiasm infectious.

"Did you know the Statue of Unity is the tallest statue in the world and is twice as tall as the Statue of Liberty?" Siya exclaimed to Vishwa, who listened with wide-eyed wonder.

Apart from the basic things needed for the trip packed by her mother in her bag, Siya packed a notepad and a few history books about Patel and Gujarat's history. She was determined to soak up every bit of it.

Vishwa, on the other hand, was more practical in his approach. He packed his clothes, favourite snacks, a cap to shield him from the sun, and a small diary to jot down his experiences.

Dharani packed her sketchbook and coloured pencils, excited to capture the beauty of Gujarat. Ajay, ever the tech enthusiast, stuffed his bag with a digital camera and portable charger.

Relieved and excited, Subhas and Sarojini packed their bags with the usual items—clothes, toiletries, and shared enthusiasm for exploration and learning. Their mother, seeing their joy, packed a few extra snacks and sweets for them to share with their friends, her heart overflowing with gratitude for the school's kindness.

As the final night before departure dawned, excitement electrified the air.

Tomorrow, the journey would begin.

Chapter 4

Into the (Un)known

The school gates buzzed with life. Parents and children mingled in a warm symphony of goodbyes.

Siya's parents hugged her and Vishwa tightly. *"Take care of each other,"* their mother urged.

Their faces glowed with excitement as they boarded the bus.

While other students waved and boarded, Sarojini stood frozen, clutching her bag. She had never been away from her father before.

Her father knelt before her, brushing a strand of hair from her face. *"My little one, it's only for a few days."*

"I know," she whispered. *"But I've never been anywhere without you."*

He exhaled softly, his eyes lingering on her for a moment. Then, with a small smile, he untied a thin, sacred thread—his taaviz—worn for protection, from his wrist and gently looped it around hers.

"Keep this taaviz with you," he murmured, his voice warm yet unsteady. *"No matter where you go, you will never be alone."*

Sarojini traced the thread with her fingers and looked up at him. *"Will it bring me back home safely?"*

Her father cupped her hands in his, squeezing gently. *"Of course."*

He hesitated for a moment, as if memorizing her face, then pulled her into a tight embrace and kissed the top of her head.

"Go now," he said, his voice quieter than before. *"Have fun!"*

Sarojini swallowed hard, nodded, and stepped onto the bus—still holding onto the thread.

Bags stowed, hands waved, and Ms. Shehnaz did a quick headcount before giving the all-clear.

Siya stole a glance at her friends, feeling her heart swell. This was more than a school trip—it was an adventure waiting to unfold.

The school arranged for a flight from Bangalore to Surat, followed by a bus journey to the Statue of Unity.

At the airport, students buzzed with excitement. Some were frequent flyers. Others, like Sarojini, clutched their bags tight.

"I've never been on a plane before," whispered Sarojini.

Subhas nodded, gripping his backpack. *"What if it shakes too much? Or—"*

"What if it falls from the sky?" He whispered.

"You'll be fine," Siya reassured them, *"Take-off is the best part!"*

Standing nearby, Ms. Shehnaz smiled and said, *"Don't worry, it's completely safe. Just follow the instructions and enjoy the view."*

The students boarded the flight, settling into their seats.

As the plane began taxiing to the runway, Subhas gripped the armrest tightly.

"This is going to be awesome," Vishwa said, grinning.

"Or terrifying," muttered Subhas.

Sarojini, sitting by the window, clutched the sacred thread on her wrist as the engines roared to life.

"Don't worry," Siya reassured her again. *"It's like a bus ride, just higher up."*

The aircraft lifted off, and Sarojini gasped as the city shrank below them.

"Look how tiny the houses are!" she marvelled quietly.

Ajay, who had seemed relaxed, suddenly tightened his grip on the seat. Dharani smirked at him.

"Still think it's just an airport?" she teased.

"Shut up."

The flight lasted just under two hours, with some kids gazing out the window while others chatted quietly. Before long, the pilot announced their descent into Surat.

"Already?" Subhas exclaimed, blinking in surprise.

"Now we switch to the bus," Ms. Shehnaz reminded them.

After collecting their bags, the students followed their teachers to the bustling airport exit where a large sleeper bus awaited.

"Whoa, this bus is huge," Ajay muttered, peeking inside.

"It has beds?!" Subhas gasped, his eyes widening as he climbed in.

"It's a sleeper bus," Siya explained, sliding into a lower berth.

Sarojini hesitated at the step, peering inside. It wasn't like any bus she was used to.

"It's like a moving hotel," Siya encouraged, smiling reassuringly at her.

Sarojini nodded slowly, adjusting her bag before settling into a seat.

With a low rumble, the bus pulled out of the airport, heading toward their destination.

As the day stretched on, the rhythmic hum of the bus lulled the children into a drowsy state.

Vishwa pressed his nose against the window. *"How many hours left?"*

Ajay smirked. *"Only a million."*

Sarojini, who had been quietly listening, perked up. *"Did you know the Statue of Unity is taller than the Qutub Minar?"*

Dharani grinned. *"I read that it's so tall that you can see it from 25 kilometres away!"*

Siya rolled her eyes playfully. *"And now we have a tour guide."*

"That's your job, not ours.", Ajay teased.

They laughed, energy high. But as the bus hummed along the highway, their voices gradually faded into yawns and murmurs, leaving only the sound of the road.

The landscape blurred past them—fields of emerald green, dusty brown villages, bursts of vibrant flowers.

Inside, the air warmed, heavy with the scent of snacks and drowsy travellers.

"So, what's the plan when we get there?" Ajay yawned, stretching.

"Eating," Vishwa mumbled sleepily, already curled up against his bag.

Dharani smiled. *"I want to sketch the statue first."*

"Ugh, you and your sketchbook," Ajay teased, playfully nudging her.

Siya glanced at them, a small smile playing on her lips. The trip has just begun, but somehow, it already felt special.

Her head bobbed gently as her eyelids grew heavier.

That evening, when the bus made a stop, the children, wrapped in the arms of sleep, remained undisturbed.

Siya, Vishwa, and their friends were the last ones to get off for dinner.

The highway was alive with activity—dozens of identical yellow buses parked side by side, their engines humming softly into the night.

The dim fluorescent glow of a roadside eatery flickered, casting long shadows.

"Which one is ours?" Dharani asked, rubbing her eyes wearily.

"That one, I think," Ajay pointed toward a bus. It looked exactly like theirs.

Still drowsy, they climbed aboard and settled into the last row, the seats feeling familiar enough not to raise questions.

The doors hissed shut. The bus pulled away.

As Siya settled into her seat, she noticed *the cushion felt... stiffer?*

She dismissed the thought. Too tired to question it. Too tired to notice. Overcome by exhaustion, they quickly slipped into a deep sleep.

It was well past midnight when a gruff voice cut through the darkness.

"End of the line—Dwarka. Everyone off."

A harsh overhead light flicked on, blinding them.

Siya stirred first, rubbing her eyes as she looked around.

Something felt wrong.

The seats were too empty.

The familiar voices of their classmates were missing.

"Where is everyone?" she murmured, feeling her stomach twist.

Dharani sat up groggily, blinking. *"What's happening?"*

Vishwa pressed his face against the window. His breath fogged up the glass.

"That's... that's not the Statue of Unity," he whispered, voice tight with fear.

A chill shot through Siya as the conductor's voice boomed again.

"Dwarka, last stop. Time to get off."

Chapter 5

Wrong Turn, Right Place

The bus rumbled into the night, leaving six children stranded. Streetlights flickered, casting long, wavering shadows.

For a moment, no one spoke.

Vishwa's small fingers clenched tightly around Siya's hand.

"Siya, where are we?" His voice was small, uncertain.

Siya's stomach twisted. She wanted to say *"Dwarka,"* but the word caught in her throat.

But how?

How had they gotten on the wrong bus?

Sarojini and Subhas held hands, silent and unsure.

Ajay rubbed his eyes, shaking off sleep. *"Okay. No need to panic. Let's just… call someone."* Him, Siya and Dharani packed phones given by their parents in their bags.

"Call? With what?" Dharani whispered.

Then, realization struck them like a punch to the gut.

"Our bags!" gasped Subhas.

They spun around, frantically searching. But their backpacks—containing their money, food, and phones—were gone, left behind on the school bus.

Siya's heart pounded.

"This can't be happening," Ajay muttered, running a hand through his hair.

Suddenly, Ajay noticed Dharani clutching a small backpack, his eyes widening as his voice rose.

"You have your bag?" he blurted out. *"If your phone isn't inside, what is?!"*

Dharani winced at the sudden attention.

"Uh… well…" she mumbled, hugging the bag closer.

Ajay stared at her, waiting.

She finally sighed. *"It's… my colouring bag,"* she admitted. *"Crayons, sketchbook… not exactly rescue tools."*

"Fantastic," Ajay said sarcastically. *"Stranded in a strange city with nothing but crayons. Maybe you can draw us a map home!"*

Dharani scowled. *"Excuse me for having hobbies."*

At that moment, two men stepped out from a narrow alley. One had a scruffy beard, the other reeked of betel and stale smoke. Their smiles didn't reach their eyes.

"You kids look lost," the bearded one said, his voice too unsettlingly smooth. *"Need some help?"*

The children stiffened.

Ajay glanced at Siya, barely moving his lips. *"Bad idea. Let's go."*

Siya nodded slightly. She didn't need to say anything—the unease in her stomach told her enough.

Without another word, they turned and started walking in the opposite direction.

Vishwa frowned, confused. *"But why aren't we taking their help?"*

Ajay didn't miss a beat. *"Yeah, let's totally follow creepy strangers into an alley. Great idea."*

Vishwa's eyes widened slightly, realization dawning. *"Oh."*

"Hey, no need to be rude," the second man called after them.

The kids walked faster.

"Strange people around here," Subhas mumbled.

"Yeah," Ajay muttered. *"Let's make sure we don't meet more of them."*

Beneath the quiet sky, something shifted. They weren't just students anymore; they were young explorers, far from home, with no map, no gear, and only each other; about to embark on an unplanned adventure.

Siya glanced at her wristwatch. 2:17 AM.

At this hour, the city of Dwarka was eerily silent.

Not a soul was in sight, save for the occasional homeless person curled up on the sidewalks, wrapped in thin blankets. The dim streetlights cast long, flickering shadows that made each narrow alley seem to lead to nowhere.

"Folks, Dwarka isn't just any city—it's Lord Krishna's city," Siya began, her voice steady yet filled with awe.

"It's one of the seven most ancient cities in India, and it's full of mysteries. They say an entire city—Krishna's original Dwarka—lies submerged beneath the sea."

She turned to face them, her eyes gleaming despite the exhaustion.

"And somewhere nearby is the Dwarkadhish Temple, a place that's stood for over 2,500 years. If there's anywhere we might find people, it would be there."

Ajay, Vishwa, Dharani, and the twins listened intently.

Siya's words lingered in the air, but before anyone could respond, she spotted something up ahead—a weathered green signpost standing under a dim streetlight.

She hurried forward, wiping the dust off the metal board with her sleeve.

"Dwarkadhish Temple – 1.1 KM →"

Her heart skipped a beat.

"Look! The temple's close!" She called to the others. *"If we follow this, we'll find someone there."*

Ajay crossed his arms, skeptical. *"What if it's empty?"*

Siya met his gaze, determined. "Then we'll figure something else out. We can't stay still."

Ajay glanced at the sign, exhaling. *"Great, just a short midnight stroll through an empty city. Totally normal."*

"At least we know where we're going," Dharani muttered, adjusting her bag.

Siya nodded; her confidence renewed. *"Come on, let's move before it gets colder."*

With that, the six of them pushed forward, their shadows stretching long under the streetlights.

Vishwa, with a sense of curiosity as vast as the night sky, looked up at his sister with wide, trusting eyes. *"Akka, could we find someone at the temple who could help us?"* he asked hopefully.

"Yes, let's hurry," Siya whispered. *"The temple is about a kilometre away; if we keep walking, we'll get there in fifteen minutes."*

"Fifteen minutes?" Vishwa groaned, dragging his feet. *"I'm so thirsty."*

"I'm hungry too," Sarojini added softly.

Siya squeezed Vishwa's hand, feeling guilt weigh on her chest—they hadn't eaten in hours.

"We'll find something soon," she assured them. *"But first, we need to get to the temple."*

They hurried along, their footsteps echoing off the empty streets.

Ajay pointed to a rusty signboard at the end of the road. *"Dwarkadhish Temple – 900m."*

"At least we're going the right way," Dharani muttered.

As they turned a corner, a welcoming sight greeted them.

Against a crumbling wall, a faded painting of Lord Krishna stood out in the darkness—flute raised, eyes kind and knowing.

And right below it, resting near his fingers, was a painted flute, pointing in the direction of the temple.

"That's…convenient," Subhas murmured.

Siya tilted her head. *"Or maybe it's a sign."*

Ajay rolled his eyes. *"Siya, it's literally a sign."*

"No, I mean…" Siya hesitated. Something about this felt different.

They walked past another intersection.

Another Lord Krishna image. Another flute. This time Siya stared and realized something strange. The flute always pointed in the direction they were meant to go.

"Okay, now this can't be a coincidence," Dharani muttered. She noticed the second Krishna image now.

"Come on, Dwaraka is Lord Krishna's city; we're bound to find his images everywhere," Ajay dismissed her concerns.

Siya stayed quiet. But inside, the feeling grew that someone—or something—was guiding them to the temple.

Vishwa yawned loudly, rubbing his eyes. His small steps were slowing.

"Siya, can we take a break?" he mumbled.

"We're almost there," she encouraged. But the truth was, even she felt the exhaustion creeping in.

A signboard came into view.

"Dwarkadhish Temple – 400m."

"Just a few more minutes," Siya said. *"We'll rest as soon as we get there."*

Sarojini leaned against Subhas, her stomach growling audibly.

Ajay rubbed his arms. *"Is it just me, or is it getting colder?"*

A sharp gust swept through the alley, rattling shutters and fluttering old posters. The wind carried something strange—salt, smoke... and something older.

Siya shivered; the temple was close.

But the silence... it felt unnaturally deep.

It was as if the city itself was holding its breath.

Then—around the bend—they saw it.

A shape in the dark. Towering. Eternal.

The past, rising in stone and moonlight.

Before them stood the Dwarkadhish Temple, rising like a guardian of time itself.

Even in the pale glow of the moon, its towering spire gleamed against the dark sky, crowned with a giant saffron flag that danced in the wind. The sheer height of the structure made them feel small, as though they had stepped into a world where legends still whispered through the stones.

Siya's breath caught in her throat.

"*It's… magnificent,*" she whispered.

Carved from golden-hued limestone, the temple's walls were adorned with intricate sculptures that seemed to whisper stories of another time. Pillars bore the figures of celestial beings, warriors, and sages, all frozen in time, their faces worn smooth by centuries of wind and devotion.

Dharani, her artistic mind overwhelmed by the detail, could barely speak.

"*The way the moonlight strikes those carvings… they look like a living painting,*" she murmured.

Ahead of them, the Swarg Dwar loomed large, its 56 ancient stone steps descending toward the silent waters of the Gomti River.

Vishwa stared up at it, wide-eyed. "*Krishna must have walked here,*" he whispered, more to himself than to anyone else.

Ajay, usually unimpressed by historical places, found himself momentarily speechless.

"*I have to admit,*" he muttered, "*this is way cooler than I expected.*"

But even amidst their awe, Ajay's instincts screamed that something was off.

The temple—one of the most famous in India—felt too empty.

No pilgrims. No distant chants. No ringing of temple bells.

The wind dropped to a still. The silence deepened further.

And then—

A low voice—too calm, too close.

"Lost, are we?"

The children screamed, their voices breaking through the night. The stillness shattered.

Chapter 6

....

The Man in the Mist

The street lay unnervingly silent, broken only by their hurried footsteps on the uneven pavement. Even the wind had stilled, as if the city itself was holding its breath.

Suddenly, a sharp crack rang out—a twig snapped somewhere behind them.

Ajay whirled around. The shadows stretched long under the dim streetlight, but nothing moved.

Then, a figure stepped forward.

The children froze as a tall figure emerged, his silhouette sharp against the flickering temple light in the distance.

"Fear not, young ones," the figure said, his voice a soothing balm in the tense night air. *"I mean you no harm."*

The man stepped forward, temple light casting long shadows across his face. His black beard was neatly trimmed, his long hair tied back. His eyes—dark yet strangely knowing—held a quiet certainty. His simple, traditional clothes seemed untouched by the dust of the streets.

He looked out of place, yet perfectly at home in the night.

"You seem lost," he said gently. *"I couldn't help but notice your distress."*

Instead of calming them, his presence sent a ripple of fear through the group.

Subhas gripped Sarojini's hand tightly, his voice trembling. *"Siya… I don't like this."*

Sarojini edged closer to Vishwa, her eyes welling with tears.

Ajay squared his shoulders. *"Who are you? Why are you following us?"* His voice was steadier than he felt. *"I don't know if you noticed, but a cop just passed us. I could call out for him."*

The man didn't flinch.

"I am sorry if I startled you. Where are my manners? Let's start again. My name is Revanth."

He smiled patiently, gesturing vaguely down the street. *"I own the fruit shop over there. I rise early to prepare fresh flowers and offerings before the temple opens."* He pointed down the road, but the dim light obscured any view of the shop he mentioned. Suspicion hung heavy in the air.

Siya's eyes narrowed. "*We don't know you,*" she said cautiously. "*We'll be fine on our own.*"

Revanth nodded, his expression thoughtful. "*You're right to be cautious. It's late, and these streets can be dangerous.*"

He reached into his bag. Instantly, Siya stiffened, Ajay stepped back, and Vishwa whimpered.

But instead of a weapon, he pulled out a deep red apple and a water bottle.

With deliberate calm, he took a slow bite.

The crisp crunch of the apple broke the silence.

He unscrewed the bottle, took a sip, and smiled.

"*See? Just a simple man with some fruit and water,*" he said with a smile. But the children didn't move.

The children exchanged uncertain looks. Dharani's lips were dry, her throat raw from thirst.

Don't take anything from strangers…

The bottle glistened in the moonlight. Droplets slid down its surface—cold, tempting. She could almost taste it.

Her fingers twitched.

Sensing their reluctance, Revanth knelt on one knee, keeping his distance. His gaze softened, as though he understood more than he was letting on.

"I know what it's like to feel lost," he said gently. *"When I was a boy, I wandered from my family during a festival. One moment I was staring at a stall of bright clay toys— and the next, they were gone. The crowd felt too big, too loud. I was terrified."*

The sincerity in his voice made the children pause. They could feel he wasn't just telling a story to make them trust him; it was as though he truly understood their fear. Vishwa tugged at Siya's sleeve. His lips were dry, his eyes big and pleading.

Siya hesitated, wanting to say yes, but…

Ajay gave her a look. A silent warning.

Finally, Siya exhaled. *"Just water,"* she said softly.

Dharani spoke up. *"If you don't mind,"* she said carefully, *"can you drink a little more? Just to be sure."*

Revanth smiled, understanding their unease. He took another sip and finished the apple, tossing the core aside. *"No tricks here—just fruits and water."*

Ajay stared at the bottle. Inside, the water glistened, cool droplets beading down the side.

His fingers hovered just above it. A strange tension filled the air.

What if—?

He shot a glance at Siya. She didn't speak, but her eyes said everything.

Ajay swallowed hard. He took two sips. That should be enough… right?

Still, his chest tightened as he picked up the bottle. He turned it over in his hands, exhaled, and finally took a cautious sip. Realizing it was safe, he passed it to Vishwa, who drank eagerly. The others followed, each taking careful sips.

Revanth placed two more bottles and several fruits on the nearby bench, then stepped back, watching quietly. The twins reached for the fruits first, and soon the others followed.

"Thank you," Siya said with a polite nod. *"We'll be on our way now."*

"At this hour? It's not safe to be out on your own," Revanth said gently. *"I can stay with you until dawn. But first—what brings such a young group to the streets of Dwarka?"*

With a hesitant glance at her friends, Siya explained everything—the school trip, the wrong bus, ending up in Dwarka. Revanth listened intently, his expression thoughtful, as if piecing together a puzzle far beyond their story.

Once they finished, Revanth nodded slowly. "I see. You've found yourselves on an unexpected adventure. Six kids from Harmony Public School—The Harmony Six, ha?" he said with a slight smile.

"*Do you have a phone?*" Siya asked cautiously. "*We need to contact our teachers.*"

Revanth nodded and pulled a phone from his pocket. Relief swept through the children. Finally—help.

"*Give me the numbers,*" he requested calmly.

Siya recited Ms. Shehnaz's number. Revanth dialled, pressing the phone to his ear.

A moment passed. Then another.

The phone rang once.

Then—the call dropped.

Revanth frowned and checked the screen. Full signal.

"*That's odd.*" he murmured, his voice calm, but thoughtful.

"*Try again!*" Ajay urged, shifting impatiently.

Revanth dialled once more. The phone rang once… then cut off again.

Ajay grabbed the phone and checked the screen.

Five full bars. Strong network.

There was no reason for the call to fail.

"This makes no sense," he muttered, frantically typing in his father's number and hitting the call button.

It rang. Once. Twice.

Then—silence. The call failed.

Ajay's frustration turned into unease. He swallowed, looking up at the others.

"We're in a city, not some deserted village," Dharani said, her voice tinged with disbelief. *"There's no way every number would fail. This… this isn't normal."*

A tense silence stretched between them.

Revanth exhaled deeply, his fingers lingering on the phone.

He remained silent for a moment, then looked up, his eyes meeting Siya's. He gazed at her intently, and something flickered in his gaze—something almost like recognition. He couldn't explain it, but there was something in her eyes, something familiar. A deep connection stirred inside him as if he had seen her before. But how? She was just a child, twelve years old, and yet...

"You," Revanth whispered, not breaking eye contact, *"I feel as though we've met before."*

Siya blinked, confused. *"What? That's not possible."*

But Revanth couldn't shake the feeling. Ancient memories stirred. Could she be connected to something long forgotten? He didn't know—but he felt it deep inside: a pull. A trust.

"Perhaps..." he murmured, more to himself than to her, then shook his head as if to dispel the thought. *"No, it can't be."*

Siya, still perplexed, asked cautiously, "What do you mean?"

Before Revanth could say more, the temple bells tolled, loud and sudden, echoing across the empty streets.

A gust of wind stirred around them, sending a faint chill through the air.

Ajay shivered. *"Okay... that was weird."*

As the temple bells tolled, Revanth's fingers absently brushed something on his right wrist. He smiled—a knowing, distant smile. Then, after a deep breath, he spoke slowly, carefully.

"Some things," he finally said, slipping the phone into his pocket. *"Are beyond technology's reach."*

The children looked at him, puzzled and nervous.

Chapter 7

....

The Man Beyond Time

"Time has a strange way of bringing people together," Revanth murmured, almost to himself.

Ajay scoffed. *"Yeah, well, time also has a strange way of making people say weird things at midnight."*

Revanth chuckled but said nothing.

Siya's gaze lingered on Revanth's right arm, where a golden, beautifully designed ornament hung—an artifact that looked extremely old.

"This is crazy," Ajay muttered, snapping Siya. *"Some guy shows up in the middle of the night talking about 'unexpected meetings', and we're just supposed to sit here and listen?"*

Dharani tried to calm Ajay down. *"Do we have a choice? Where else can we go?"*

Siya hesitated. Every instinct told her to be cautious—but Revanth seemed trustworthy. And what other option did they have?

She exhaled. *"Relax, we won't let our guard down."*

Ajay wasn't convinced—but he said nothing.

The temple bells tolled once more, their chime rolling through the quiet streets.

Revanth's gaze lingered on Siya a moment too long. It wasn't just curiosity—there was something else.

"You look at me as if you know me," she said cautiously.

Revanth blinked, as if snapping himself from a thought. Then, with a small smile, he said,

"Maybe I do."

The children exchanged uneasy glances.

"Okay, what does that even mean?" Ajay scoffed. *"One minute you talk like some wise old man, and the next you act like you've met Siya before?"*

"Not her," Revanth said, his tone unreadable. *"Not exactly. I'm not sure myself."*

Siya's breath caught for just a second.

"Enough with the riddles," Dharani interrupted. *"Can you please help us, or at least guide us to the police station?"*

Revanth exhaled and gestured toward the grand Dwarkadhish Temple, standing tall in the moonlight.

"Tell me... what do you know about Dwarka?"

The question took them by surprise.

"Dwarka?" Vishwa repeated.

"We know it was Krishna's city," Dharani said hesitantly. *"And that it sank under the sea. At least that's what Siya said."*

Siya jumped into the conversation, *"That's what I read in the History books."*

Revanth smiled faintly, but there was something almost sad about it.

"That's what the books say," he murmured, almost to himself.

The children waited, sensing he had more to say.

"But tell me this—have you ever wondered why Dwarka was the only great city to disappear completely? Why no traces of its glory remain—no temples, no palaces, no streets?"

"Because it's underwater," Ajay replied flatly. *"Obviously."*

Revanth shook his head.

"No," he said simply. *"It's because it was meant to disappear."*

A strange silence settled over them.

"Meant to?" Siya echoed, frowning.

"Dwarka didn't just sink because of natural disasters," Revanth continued, his gaze drifting toward the temple's

towering silhouette. *"It did, yes. But not in the way you think. It happened through forces greater than we can comprehend."*

Dharani's eyes widened. *"You mean… the gods?"*

"That," Revanth concluded, *"is a story for another day."*

A frustrated frown tugged at Siya's face. Though she couldn't pinpoint why, she felt drawn to listen further.

"So, where do you get all this?" Ajay asked, arms crossed. *"The Puranas? Old legends?"*

Revanth turned his gaze toward Ajay then, holding it steady.

"No."

The single word sent a strange chill down Siya's spine.

"I know because I saw it happen."

The words fell like a heavy stone into a still lake.

Ajay let out a sharp laugh, breaking the silence. *"Oh, come on. You saw it happen? Right. Of course. You're what… thousands of years old now?"*

Revanth's expression remained unshaken, untouched by the sarcasm. His voice, when he spoke, was steady—like someone who had long made peace with the burden of his knowledge.

"Time isn't as rigid as you think, young one," he said, his tone neither defensive nor boastful. *"There are those who witness history not from pages, but from life itself."*

Ajay opened his mouth to argue, but something about Revanth's unwavering gaze made him hesitate.

"I did not read about Dwarka's final days," Revanth continued. *"I remember them."*

"I watched as the sea rose—not in fury or by chance, but with deliberate purpose. I witnessed a city destined to stand forever... yet it was forced to disappear."

A strange, heavy silence settled among them.

The air around them seemed to still. The children, unsure of what was coming, leaned in slightly, waiting for him to continue.

Revanth looked into Siya's eyes once more, feeling that deep connection, and decided it was time.

The children stood in stunned silence, grappling with Revanth's claim. Ajay's skepticism was palpable, arms crossed tightly. Dharani and the younger ones exchanged uncertain glances, while Siya felt an inexplicable pull toward Revanth's words.

Revanth observed their reactions, his gaze lingering on each of them before settling on Siya. *"I understand your doubts,"* he began, his voice calm and steady. *"But allow me to share a story—one that transcends the boundaries of time."*

Revanth took a deep breath, drawing strength from past memories. *"In an age forgotten by most, there lived a king named Raivata Kakudmi, who ruled the prosperous city of Kushasthali. His daughter, Revati, was unparalleled in grace and beauty. Seeking wisdom beyond books or advisors, he and Revati journeyed to the heavens—to the abode of Lord Brahma, the Creator, for his guidance. The king believed the journey would also help him find a suitor worthy of his daughter."*

The children listened intently, the ancient names and tales stirring something deep within them.

"Time flows differently in divine realms," Revanth continued. *"What seemed like mere moments to Kakudmi and his daughter Lord Brahma's abode were, in truth, ages upon ages on Earth. When they returned, their world had transformed beyond recognition. Their city, their people—all had changed. It was then that Revati was wed to Lord Balarama, the brother of Lord Krishna."*

"Science is catching up, now calling it 'Time Dilation'— you'd know this if you've watched the movie - 'Interstellar'," he added.

Ajay, the Sci-Fi expert, seemed to start believing what Revanth was saying. He'd watched *Interstellar* several times.

Siya's eyes widened as the pieces of the ancient puzzle aligned in her mind. "*But... what does this have to do with you?*" she asked, her voice barely above a whisper.

Revanth's gaze softened, and a bittersweet smile touched his lips. "*I,*" he said, his voice calm yet strong, "*am Raivata Kakudmi.*" He revealed gently, "*I've walked through the corridors of time, witnessing the rise and fall of civilizations, the ebb and flow of human endeavour.*"

The revelation hung in the air, heavy and surreal. Ajay's skepticism faltered, replaced by a flicker of uncertainty. Dharani's eyes widened in awe, while the younger ones seemed caught between disbelief and fascination.

Siya felt a shiver run down her spine. "*But... how is that possible?*" she asked, her voice trembling as her mind raced to comprehend the enormity of his confession.

Revanth nodded, acknowledging their disbelief. "*Time is a vast ocean, filled with currents beyond our understanding,*" he explained. "*My quest for wisdom and a worthy suitor for my daughter led me to realms where time flows differently. Upon returning, I found that centuries had passed, and the world I knew had vanished beneath the waves of change.*"

The children absorbed his words, their understanding of reality stretching to accommodate the extraordinary tale unfolding before them.

Revanth's expression grew contemplative, as if weighing a decision. *"I understand that words alone may not convey the truth of my tale,"* he said. *"Trust is earned. Perhaps it's time I show you."*

He extended his right hand, palm up, holding the ornament on his wrist with his left hand, beginning to chant softly.

The words were unlike anything the children had ever heard—ancient, rhythmic, resonating with power that transcended time.

The very air around them seemed to quiver, as if the world itself were inhaling. A faint glow pulsed at his fingertips, spreading outward in shimmering waves.

And then—

A thin, golden arc materialized, suspended like liquid light. It widened, stretching and bending, as if reality itself were unfolding, peeling apart at the seams.

With a soft hum, the space inside the arc rippled—not empty, not solid, but something ethereal. The surface of the portal shimmered like sunlight dancing on ocean waves, yet beneath it lay a depth that seemed endless, infinite.

It was neither a door nor a window, yet it called to them, like the whisper of an untold story eager to be revealed.

The golden edges pulsed, shifting in hue from deep sapphire to violet and then back to gold, as if the portal were alive.

The children stared, breathless with awe.

Ajay took a step back, the glow casting sharp shadows across his face. Dharani clutched her bag tighter, her fingers trembling. Siya felt a pull toward it, as if a forgotten memory was brushing against her soul.

"What... is that?" Subhas whispered, his voice barely audible above the wind.

Revanth simply smiled and stepped into the portal.

Chapter 8

Echoes Through Eternity

The children gasped as Revanth vanished before their eyes, his form dissolving into a thousand points of light. Frozen, they scanned the space around them, unsure of where he had gone. No one dared approach the mysterious portal that had swallowed him whole.

Suddenly, the air behind them shimmered, a low hum vibrating through the ground. As if painted by an invisible hand, a second portal unfurled like liquid gold, and from within, Revanth stepped out, completely unharmed, his smile as enigmatic as ever.

"*Magic!*" Vishwa exclaimed, his voice a blend of delight and disbelief, nearly stumbling backward in his excitement.

The twins clutched each other, hands covering their mouths, eyes wide with wonder. Siya's breath caught in her throat as she tried to piece together the impossible. Even Ajay, the perpetual skeptic, felt his doubts waver under the weight of what he'd just witnessed.

"*How... how is that possible?*" Dharani whispered, her disbelief mirroring that of the group.

Revanth extended a calming hand. *"I know this is overwhelming,"* he said softly, the light from the portal casting flickering shadows across his face. *"Come, let's sit here and talk."* He gestured towards a bench by the temple's grand entrance.

For a moment, no one moved. The children exchanged nervous glances. *"But—what exactly is that?!"* Ajay finally burst out, pointing at the still-glowing portal.

"A door," Revanth said simply. *"To realms beyond your wildest imaginations, to places where few dare to tread."*

A shiver ran down Siya's spine. She wanted to ask more, but Revanth had already turned toward the stone bench, the weight of centuries pressing against its weathered surface. After a moment's hesitation, she followed him, and one by one, the others trailed behind. With a wave of his hand, Revanth closed the portal.

The children sat in stunned silence. Sarojini clutched Subhas' arm, her breaths shallow and quick, while Dharani's eyes remained wide, filled with awe. Ajay rubbed his eyes, as if trying to erase an illusion.

Siya exhaled slowly, her head shaking slightly in disbelief. *"I—I don't even know what to say. But I believe you now,"* she murmured, her voice low and apologetic.

Revanth sighed, a sound heavy with the weight of centuries. *"At first, I was lost. My daughter was married to Lord Balarama, and I was overjoyed for her. But when*

I returned to my kingdom, I found myself adrift—a relic of a world that no longer recognized my name, forgotten by time itself." He closed his eyes, momentarily lost in that moment of profound despair.

"*Lord Brahma saw my plight,*" Revanth continued, his voice a whisper of its former strength." *He appeared to me again, not in his celestial abode, but right here, on this very land.*"

Subhas leaned in, his breath held in suspense. "*Did... did he help you?*"

Revanth nodded slowly. "*He did. But not as I had anticipated. He granted me a boon—a gift, yet a burden. I was given the ability to journey through time and space, to witness history unfold, to absorb wisdom from the ages. But it came at a cost.*"

His voice faltered, tinged with sorrow.

Dharani shifted uneasily, her fingers twisting the hem of her shirt. "*What... What was the cost?*"

Revanth's eyes met hers, calm yet carrying the weight of eternity. "*Eternal life.*"

A hush fell over the group.

"*I was granted the power to walk through the ages, never perishing. But there was a condition—I could not look the same. People would notice if I never aged, if I never grew old like they did.*"

Vishwa's eyes widened. *"So... you don't get old?"*

Revanth's smile was faint, tinged with emotion difficult to decipher. *"Not as you do. Instead, I can alter my appearance, age as necessary, blending seamlessly into the world around me. And when the time is right, I depart— shedding one identity, reverting to youth, and beginning anew elsewhere."*

Ajay blinked, his mind struggling to grasp the enormity of what he was hearing. *"So you just... live forever? You change how you look and no one realizes?"*

Revanth nodded slowly. *"Yes. For centuries, I have walked this Earth, witnessing kingdoms rise and fall, experiencing time in ways you can't imagine. I've adopted countless identities, assumed numerous forms—but inside, I remain the same. And although I can appear to grow old... I never truly die."*

The wind rustled softly around them, as if the air itself were holding its breath, hanging on his every word.

Sarojini, finally spoke, her voice barely a whisper. *"Isn't it... lonely? Living like that? Watching everyone else grow old and leave?"*

Revanth's smile faded, replaced by a somber expression. His fingers traced the edge of the ancient golden ornament on his wrist, his grip tightening as if holding onto something long lost. The ornament, called a *Kāda*, was beautifully ornate, engraved with symbols of the

Shankha (Conch), Padma (Lotus), Trishul (Trident), and Kālachakra (Wheel of Time).

"Yes," he admitted softly. *"It is a heavy burden. I have watched many I cared for pass on while I remain. But it is the path I chose—one that I must continue to walk."*

For a long moment, silence enveloped them. His words hung heavy in the air, creating a sense of quiet unease.

Then, as if drawn by a force greater than himself, Revanth's gaze drifted toward the towering spire of the temple. The flickering moonlight played across the sharp angles of his face, making him look like a man who had lived through legends and lifetimes alike.

"But among all the lives I have lived, there is one I will never forget—the years I spent in the city of Dwarka."

The children sat frozen, their hearts pounding in the heavy silence.

"I had the fortune—the immense blessing—of walking beside Lord Krishna in this very city," Revanth began, his voice imbued with reverence. *"I saw his wisdom, his laughter, his boundless kindness. I witnessed his miracles unfold before my own eyes. I watched this city flourish under his rule—its golden domes rising to the skies, its streets alive with music, trade, and fervent devotion to Lord Krishna."*

His voice, steady and deep, echoed with the essence of a bygone era that lived on within him.

"I saw Krishna guide his people through times of war and peace. And in the quiet moments, I watched him play his flute at sunset, his gaze lost in a world only he could see and understand."

His voice faltered, a tremor of loss passing through his words.

"And then... I witnessed it all sink beneath the waves."

A cold hush fell over the group. Even Ajay, who had been skeptical just moments earlier, found himself speechless.

Siya swallowed hard. *"You saw Dwarka sink?"*

Revanth nodded, his expression unreadable. He held the moment for a beat longer, then exhaled, as if shaking himself free from the memory.

"Yes. And that is a story for another time."

The gravity in his voice hinted at layers yet untold—there was more to tell, stories far more than the night could hold.

But he did not dwell on these thoughts. His expression shifted, composed once more. He straightened slightly, his voice steadied, bringing himself back to the present.

The children remained silent, captivated by Revanth's extraordinary tale. The night around them seemed to pulse with life—not only from the rustling wind but also from the echoes of a past too vast to fully comprehend.

Siya, her voice filled with a mix of wonder and uncertainty, was the first to break the silence. *"So, you've seen history unfold? The rise and fall of empires, the birth of civilizations?"*

Revanth nodded solemnly. *"Yes. I have witnessed the tapestry of time in all its glory... and its sorrow."*

He glanced toward the temple, its ancient stones standing firm against the ages, as if carrying the weight of history within them. His voice was steady, yet distant—as if he were not merely recalling the past, but seeing it unfold before his eyes.

"I have stood at the edge of the battlefields of Kurukshetra, watching as fate determined the course of a war that shaped the soul of this land." His gaze darkened. *"I walked through the bustling streets of Harappa, where knowledge and trade blossomed long before the world knew their names. I witnessed India's temples rise as beacons of faith and wisdom—only to see them fall under the onslaught of invaders, their sacred idols shattered, their walls scarred by time and destruction."*

His fingers brushed absently against his wrist ornament, the *Kāda,* a silent reminder of the eras he had lived through.

"I witnessed the splendor of the Mughal Empire, its rise etched in blood and power, its decline written in betrayal. I was there when the first sparks of rebellion ignited in

the hearts of those who braved to dream of a free India. And I stood among the crowds when, after centuries of struggle, this land reclaimed its independence—its spirit unbroken, its people triumphant."

The air hung heavy with unspoken thoughts after he unveiled the passage of centuries.

"But we are not here to linger on the past," he said, his gaze shifting and settling intently on Siya. *"We are here because of you."*

Siya straightened slightly, her expression a mix of confusion and curiosity.

"Some force drew me toward you," he continued, then glanced at the others. *"All of you."* The children exchanged uncertain glances, the air thick with anticipation.

"Looks like you could use some help," he said, a small smile curling the corners of his lips. *"And as it happens... I am in a position to offer it."*

He paused, then lifted his right wrist, letting his fingers to rest gently on the golden ornament—the Kālachakra Kāda that shimmered under the moonlight. His eyes fluttered closed for a brief moment.

Then, he chanted softly, his voice carrying an ancient rhythm.

The air shifted. The space before them rippled as if touched by an unseen force.

A new portal unfurled, its light gleaming like molten gold, swirling with potent energy. The children stared in awe, the magnitude of his words finally sinking in.

"This is no ordinary doorway," he said. *"Through these portals, I walk through time itself. They grant me passage to any place, any era. The past, the present, the future—they all lie within my reach."*

The children stared, mesmerized by the swirling vortex of light, fully absorbing the implications of his revelation.

"And right now," Revanth continued, a glimmer of amusement in his eyes, *"I believe you need to be back on your bus. Conveniently, I can take you exactly where you were supposed to be—just as you were about to step off at the Statue of Unity."*

A stunned silence followed.

"Wait... you can do that?" Ajay finally asked, his voice laced with a mix of disbelief and curiosity.

Revanth chuckled. *"I wouldn't offer if I couldn't,"* he replied, his eyes twinkling.

The portal shimmered, its golden light swirling as if alive, beckoning them closer. The children stared, awe-struck, as the gateway to the unimaginable lay open before them—waiting for their decision.

Chapter 9

Past Tense? Present Tense?

The golden light of the portal from the Kālachakra Kāda flickered, casting dancing shadows across the temple walls. The children stood silent, captivated not only by Revanth's revelations but also by the mesmerizing swirl of the portal.

Finally, Siya turned to Ajay with a teasing grin. *"Well, looks like we're finally going back to learning history."*

Ajay groaned dramatically, throwing his hands in the air. *"Seriously? After everything we've just heard and seen, you're bringing up history? That's the most boring—"*

"Boring?" Revanth interrupted, his voice sharp with amusement. He folded his arms and tilted his head, a knowing smile tugging at his lips.*" Are you suggesting that tales of epic battles, lost cities, and ancient legends are... boring?"*

Caught off guard, Ajay hesitated. *"I mean... yeah? Memorizing dates and reading old stories? Not exactly thrilling."*

Revanth's smile widened. He tapped the Kālachakra Kāda on his wrist, and for a brief moment, the Kāda flared with a pulse of energy, as if reacting to his thoughts, and closed the existing portal.

"Then why don't you stop reading about history... and live it?"

Ajay blinked, taken aback. *"Wait, what?"*

Siya's teasing expression shifted to one of genuine curiosity. *"What do you mean by that?"*

Revanth stepped forward, his voice smooth and filled with an air of mystery. *"What if, instead of merely flipping through pages in a book, you could walk the streets of ancient cities? Witness history unfolding before your very eyes? See legends take shape and change the world?"*

The children gasped. Dharani clutched her sketchbook bag, her fingers twitching as if she could already visualize the worlds Revanth was painting with his words.

"You mean... we could actually go there?" Vishwa whispered, his voice quivering with excitement.

Revanth's eyes twinkled mischievously. *"Oh, you have no idea,"* he chuckled.

He chanted once more, his fingers tracing the intricate designs of the Kālachakra Kāda. The portal responded, its swirling golden light intensifying, pulsating with energy—as if eager for them to take the next step.

Revanth's eyes glimmered with an otherworldly light. *"Indeed. I can take you directly to your teachers, or we can embark on a journey through different moments in history first. Trust me, you'll arrive at the Statue of Unity precisely when your school bus does. No one will even realize you were gone."*

"But this is not a decision to take lightly. This journey will change how you see the world, your country, its history, and perhaps even yourselves."

Dharani, her artistic soul always drawn to the mysteries of the past, asked eagerly, *"Can we really see all of that? The ancient cities, the great battles, the leaders and heroes of our past?"*

"Yes," Revanth replied, *"but it's more than just witnessing. You will experience the very essence of those times— the emotions, the struggles, the victories. It will be an adventure both marvellous and challenging."*

Subhas, his initial fear now replaced by excitement, bounced on the tips of his toes. *"Can we see dinosaurs?"* he asked, his voice bursting with the unbridled enthusiasm typical of a curious child.

Revanth chuckled softly. *"The portals of time have their limits. Yet human history brims with moments just as enthralling as the age of dinosaurs."* He paused, then added with a playful smile, *"But yes—if you truly wish, we can certainly take a quick detour."*

Subhas' face lit up with joy—and so did Vishwa's.

Sarojini, still clinging to her brother, looked up at Revanth with wide, tear-filled eyes. *"Will it be safe? I just want to go back to my parents,"* she whispered, her voice trembling.

Revanth knelt down to be eye-level with her, his expression sincere and comforting. *"I will be right by your side,"* he assured her, *"and I promise to protect you as if you were my own. This journey will be safe, yet it will also be an adventure like no other."*

The children exchanged glances; their initial anxiety now mixed with rising excitement. They were standing at the brink of an extraordinary expedition—one that would carry them through the pages of history. One by one, they nodded, silently agreeing to step into the unknown.

Siya turned toward Revanth, and suddenly something clicked. *"We're visiting the Statue of Unity, right? We were supposed to learn about Sardar Patel today,"* she said.

"What if... instead of just hearing about him in a lecture, we actually saw his life unfold? Like, really saw it?"

Ajay snorted in disbelief. *"What, like Patel ji himself, is going to give us a history lesson?"*

Revanth raised an eyebrow, impressed. *"You're thinking like a true seeker of knowledge, Siya. That's exactly where we should go."*

He turned to Ajay and said, *"Not exactly him giving a lesson, but what if you could witness history as it truly happened? See Patel ji's struggles, his choices, the moments that shaped India—exactly as they unfolded?"*

The children froze, their minds racing with the possibilities.

"You mean... we could actually be there?" Dharani asked breathlessly.

"See him free India?" Vishwa added, eyes gleaming.

"Watch history happen right in front of us?" Ajay muttered, more to himself than to anyone else.

Revanth's gaze swept across them, his face a mask of contemplation. Then, with a small smile, he tapped the Kālachakra Kāda on his wrist.

"Would that make history less boring for you?" he teased, his voice laced with knowing amusement.

Ajay opened his mouth, then shut it. For the first time, he had no sarcastic comeback.

Siya turned to the others, her heart racing. *"Then that's where we should go. Before we return to our teachers and friends, let's witness Patel ji's life unfold—with our own eyes."*

Revanth's smile widened, his eyes glowing with ancient wisdom. *"Very well, then. Brace yourselves—we are about to step directly into the pages of history."*

The portal roared to life, its golden swirls accelerating, as if sensing the gravity of the moment. It pulsed and shimmered, alive with anticipation for the journey about to begin.

Taking a collective breath, the Harmony Six—led by Revanth—stepped forward.

One by one, they crossed the threshold into the swirling light, embarking on a journey that would forever change their understanding of the world—and their place within it.

....

Chapter 10

Between the Pages of Time

The portal, a mesmerizing kaleidoscope of light and shadow, seemed to pulsate with the heartbeat of time itself.

Ajay stepped through first, and as the othersfollowed, they felt a peculiar sensation—like layers of history were wrapping around them, pulling them gently into its depths. The colours around them shifted and swirled, mingling past with present in a captivating dance of hues.

Vishwa's eyes widened in pure wonder, and Sarojini, overwhelmed by the spectacle, gripped Subhas's hand tightly.

"It's like we're in a sci-fi movie!" Ajay exclaimed, his earlier skepticism completely overshadowed by the undeniable marvel unfolding before them.

Dharani, her eyes reflecting the portal's ethereal light, whispered, *"It's more beautiful than anything anyone ever drew."*

Revanth, their guide through this extraordinary journey, deftly manipulated the portal with intricate hand movements. *"Each fold in time and space has its own resonance,"* he explained. *"I tune into the era we need to visit, like finding the right note in a vast symphony."*

Despite the enchantment surrounding them, Sarojini's hesitation lingered. Though she had agreed to follow, her fingers trembled slightly, and her tear-streaked face looked to Siya and Ajay as if pleading to turn back.

Noticing her discomfort, Siya paused, torn between her curiosity and her sense of responsibility. *"Maybe we should just get back to the teachers,"* she suggested softly.

Revanth's expression softened as he turned to Sarojini. *"I understand your concerns,"* he said gently. *"I promise you, you will be safe. Should you ever wish to return at any point, I will take you back immediately. Your safety is my responsibility."*

The kindness in his voice reassured her. The unique opportunity to learn about Sardar Patel in such anextraordinary and immersive way was too compelling to pass up. She glanced at Siya and Ajay again, her expression uncertain but no longer afraid.

"Alright," Siya said, her voice firm with newfound determination. *"Let's go on this journey. We want to learn—to truly understand who Sardar Patel was. Ajay - do you think this is okay?"*

Ajay, caught between his awe of the portal and the gravity of their situation, nodded affirmatively.

"*Excellent choice,*" said Revanth, his voice echoing with the wisdom of ages. "*Let the journey through time begin.*"

He surveyed their surroundings thoughtfully, as if trying to pinpoint the precise moment in history to introduce them to.

Siya, considering that the younger ones—Vishwa, Subhas, and Sarojini—might not be familiar with Sardar Patel's history, turned to Revanth. "*Could we start at the very beginning, with Patel ji's childhood? I think it's important for all of us to understand where and how his journey began.*"

Revanth's eyes glimmered with appreciation. "*A wise choice indeed. Understanding the roots of a person is key to comprehending the entirety of their life's journey.*"

Just as Revanth was about to initiate the portal with a swirl of his hands, Ajay interrupted with a raised hand.

"*Wait a second. If we're really going back in time, what about our cameras? Our phones? How are we supposed to record this?*"

Revanth turned to him, his expression serene but firm. "*Ah, an important question. I should have actually started with this. Let me be clear—there are rules.*"

The children exchanged glances.

"*Rules?*" Siya asked.

Revanth nodded, his silhouette framed by the flickering light of the portal.

"Time is a delicate fabric. We may walk through history, but we must never alter its weave. We cannot interact with historical figures, we cannot influence the events, and most crucially—" he paused, letting his words sink in, *"we cannot take anything from the past with us, nor leave anything behind."*

Ajay's face fell. *"No cameras? No photos? Not even a quick selfie with Patel ji?"*

Revanth chuckled, shaking his head. *"Not even that. This is not a school trip, Ajay. We are observers, nothing more. We must ensure that History remains undisturbed—at any cost."*

There was a seriousness in his voice that silenced them all. Even Ajay, who had been half-joking, swallowed hard.

Dharani's eyes sparkled with an idea. *"I can still sketch what I see, though, right?"* she asked excitedly. *"I'll just tell everyone I imagined it from what I've read!"*

Revanth chuckled, clearly impressed. *"I believe I've found great company this time around. Your art will indeed be a gift, Dharani—crafted from your imagination, inspired by history you witness."*

Vishwa and Subhas, however, had a different concern.

"But… can we at least bring our snacks?" Vishwa asked, his voice hopeful.

"And a change of clothes?!" Subhas added quickly. *"If we're going to time travel, we don't want to wear the same dusty uniforms the whole time!"*

Hearing this, Revanth could not suppress a grin.

"That, I can do."

He took a step back and, with a dramatic wave of his hand, another door appeared inside the portal. It shimmered like liquid gold, its frame radiating a welcoming glow.

"Give me just a moment."

Without further explanation, Revanth stepped through the mysterious door and vanished.

The children gasped.

"Did he just—?" Ajay began, but before he could finish, the door shimmered again, and Revanth stepped back through—holding bags filled with their belongings, minus the cameras and phones.

"Here you go," he said, handing them their things. *"Your cameras and phones, however, stay behind. Trust me, the best way to remember history is to experience it—not to take pictures of it."*

The children looked down at their bags and then up at Revanth. It wasn't just a matter of their things being returned—it was a gesture of trust.

Siya nodded slowly, absorbing the significance of the moment. "*Alright. We're ready.*"

"*Now,*" Revanth continued, his voice returning to its usual warmth, "*we're truly ready. Shall we?*"

Revanth suddenly snapped his fingers, shaking his head with a chuckle. "*Ah! I nearly forgot one more thing. Maybe old age is finally catching up with me.*"

Ajay smirked. "*Wait, can that even happen to you?*"

Revanth laughed but then his expression turned solemn as he looked at each of them. "*Jokes aside, there's one last rule—and it's the most important of all.*"

The children fell silent as Revanth's words filled the air. "*You must never reveal to anyone that you've travelled through time. If you do,*" he paused, his voice dropping to a near whisper, "*you will never see me again—and you will never be able to live these moments again.*"

The weight of his words settled over them like a heavy cloak. The thrill of adventure still pulsed in their veins, but now it carried an undeniable responsibility—one that they had not anticipated.

The children exchanged glances, their earlier excitement now mixed with the sharp edge of caution. Slowly, one by one, they nodded, a shared understanding passing between them. This journey would remain theirs alone—a secret wrapped in the folds of time itself.

Chapter 11

Seeds of Strength:
The Early Years

"Now, we are ready! Let's go!" Revanth said, his voice ringing with excitement.

He swirled his hand through the cascading lights, fingers brushing against the air as though he were pulling something from beyond the veil. With a sly wink at Siya—almost as if he had read her thoughts—he reached out and grasped the shimmering air, pulling it toward him.

A door materialized before them, its frame shifting like liquid gold. As it creaked open, a sepia-toned canvas unfurled before their eyes—a landscape where soft hues blended into one another, like the faded pages of a forgotten story, creating a dreamlike, timeless scene.

The children paused, hesitant, their eyes drinking in the surreal sight.

Revanth stepped forward first, his form blending seamlessly into the sepia hues, as if he were an old photograph coming to life.

One by one, the children followed, their steps tentative but eager.

The moment they crossed the threshold, everything changed.

A gust of warm wind swept over them, carrying the scent of earth, fresh hay, and a faint trace of smoke from a distant hearth. The sounds of cattle lowing, wooden cartwheels creaking on the dirt roads, and the joyful laughter of children echoed around them.

Ajay spun around, his jaw slightly slack. Above them, the sky stretched wide and blue, dotted with a few lazy, drifting clouds.

"Whoa," he murmured, his voice full of wonder. *"This is nothing like the India we know."*

"That's because it isn't," Revanth replied, his smile widening. *"Welcome to Gujarat. The year is 1887."*

Vishwa, never one to hold back his excitement, dashed ahead a few steps before stopping abruptly. His eyes widened.

"Look!" he cried, pointing to a small wooden sign ahead.

Its letters were roughly carved: *Welcome to Nadiad.*

Subhas, catching up, gasped softly, *"Wow!"* His eyes sparkled with awe as he looked at their surroundings.

As the children stood there, absorbing the unfamiliar sights, Dharani frowned, her fingers adjusting the strap of her bag. *"Something feels... different,"* she muttered under her breath.

Ajay looked down at himself—and froze.

"What the—?!"

Instead of their modern school uniforms, each of them was now dressed in clothing from the past.

Vishwa was now wearing a simple white cotton dhoti with a short kurta, while Ajay and Subhas had similar outfits. Their feet were bare, except for simple handwoven sandals, the kind one would expect in a village from a century ago.

The girls had transformed as well. Siya now wore a light beige ghagra with a choli and a delicate odhani draped over her shoulders. Dharani and Sarojini had similar outfits in earthy tones, their hair loosely braided, completing the look of women from another time.

Siya ran her hands over the soft fabric, her eyes wide in disbelief. *"When did this happen?!"* she exclaimed, still trying to process the change.

"I didn't even feel it!" Subhas added, spinning in a circle to better examine his own clothes.

Revanth grinned, clearly enjoying their surprise. *"You'd stand out a little too much in your uniforms, wouldn't you?"*

Ajay tugged at the edge of his dhoti with a frown. "*Did you really have to take our shoes too?*" he muttered, clearly unimpressed.

"*I only help you blend in,*" Revanth replied smoothly. "*Trust me, you'll thank me when we start walking on the dusty village roads.*"

Siya couldn't help but laugh at Ajay's exaggerated scowl, but her expression quickly turned serious as her gaze swept across the village. "So... *we can actually touch things here? Eat, drink, talk to people?*"

Revanth nodded. "*Yes. This isn't a dream or a hologram. Everything you experience here is real. People can see you, hear you, and interact with you just as they would in your own time. But remember*"—his voice lowered slightly—"*you must not say or do anything that could change history.*"

Ajay, clearly skeptical, bent down and scooped up a handful of dry soil, letting it sift through his fingers. His eyes widened in surprise.

"*It's real,*" he muttered.

Dharani reached out and ran her fingers along the rough wooden post of the Nadiad sign, tracing the grooves of the carved letters.

"*This is insane,*" she whispered, her voice filled with wonder.

Revanth chuckled softly. "*And this,*" he said, gesturing toward the bustling village, "*is just the beginning.*"

He paused for a moment, his gaze sweeping over the scene before him. "*This,*" he said, "*is where the journey of one of India's greatest leaders begins.*"

Siya, taking in the rustic homes, the dusty yet vibrant roads, and the people in traditional attire, murmured, "*So this is where Patel ji was born...*"

Revanth nodded. "*Yes. Sardar Vallabhbhai Patel was born in this very village on October 31, 1875, into a simple farmer's family. His childhood was simple, yet deeply rooted in the values that would one day shape him into the man India would call its 'Iron Man.'*"

Siya listened intently, absorbing every detail. Vishwa, curious, piped up, "*Was he a good student? Did he like to play like us?*"

"*Determined and focused,*" Revanth answered. "*Sardar Patel's early life was not one of privilege but of perseverance. He valued education and was known for his strong will and sharp mind.*"

Ajay glanced around at the rustic village setting—the mud-brick houses, the dry, cracked earth, the villagers moving about their evening chores. His expression grew more serious, his mind deep in thought.

"How did a boy from such a simple background grow up to be such an important leader?"

"That," said Revanth with a smile, *"is exactly what we are here to discover."*

Dharani, her artist's eye absorbing the world around her, felt a quiet thrill. The earthy colours of the village, the slant of the golden sunlight against the fields, the rhythmic motions of daily life—all of it told a story. She wished she could capture not just the visuals but the essence of the moments that had moulded one of India's greatest leaders.

The warm evening breeze carried the scent of freshly tilled soil, the distant aroma of woodsmoke, and the crisp, earthy fragrance of neem trees. As the sun sank lower, the village hummed with quiet activity—oxen plodding steadily along the dusty paths, children running barefoot between houses, women drawing water from a well.

The children followed Revanth as he led them deeper into the village, his voice smooth yet steady, like someone telling a story he had witnessed firsthand.

"You see," Revanth said, gesturing toward a modest, thatched-roof house in the distance. *"Vallabhbhai Patel was born to a simple farmer's family. His childhood, though filled with hard work, was deeply rooted in*

values that would eventually shape him into the man he became—resilient, disciplined, and unwavering."

As they moved forward, their footsteps stirring small clouds of dust, they saw him.

A young boy, no older than twelve, stood in the middle of a vast field, skilfully guiding two strong oxen through the rich soil. The even rhythm of his movements, the firm grip he had on the plough, and the way he steered the animals with quiet authority all spoke of a boy who had performed this task countless times before.

His simple cotton dhoti and kurta were dusted with soil, but he didn't seem to mind. The late afternoon sun gleamed off the fine sheen of sweat on his brow, yet there was no sign of fatigue, no hesitation in his work.

There was something about him—an unspoken strength, a quiet determination—that made him seem older than his years.

"That's Vallabhbhai Patel," Revanth said softly. *"Even at this age, he helps his family in the fields, never once complaining about it."*

The children stood in silence, watching as Vallabhbhai expertly guided the plough, his eyes steady and his expression one of deep concentration. He worked with such confidence that it seemed as though the earth itself obeyed his movements.

When he finally finished, he wiped the sweat from his brow with the back of his hand and led the oxen to a shaded spot by a large neem tree. With practiced ease, he unfastened their harnesses, letting them rest.

Then, without a second thought, he reached into a small cloth bag tied at his waist, pulling out a stack of rough, handmade paper and a small piece of charcoal.

Settling himself beneath the tree, his posture straight, his expression intense, he immediately began working through math problems, his focus unbroken.

The transition from labour to learning was seamless, almost as if the two parts of his life existed in harmony. The children stood in awe, watching him in silent admiration.

"Even after all that work, he's studying," Dharani whispered, admiration filling her voice.

Revanth's eyes glowed with quiet pride. *"Yes. Vallabhbhai loved learning, even when life was hard. He knew that education would be his path to making a difference."*

Ajay, still watching in disbelief, muttered under his breath, *"We complain about so many things—our parents not getting us the latest phone, school being too hard, having to wake up early. But look at him... He's using a piece of charcoal, and he's just as focused as any of us. Maybe even more."*

Subhas, noticing the tired set of Vallabhbhai's shoulders, whispered, *"Maybe we could help him with the fieldwork, so he could have more time to study."*

"Or at least give him my pencils and notebooks," Sarojini added eagerly, her eyes filled with a sense of compassion.

Before any of them could move, Revanth's calm but firm voice interrupted. *"Before you do anything, you must understand something very important."*

The children froze, sensing the change in his tone.

Revanth's eyes bore into each of them, his voice steady and unwavering. *"Interfering with the past, no matter how small, can have serious consequences on the future."* He let the gravity of his words sink in, the silence pressing heavily on them. *"A single action can create ripples, altering events in ways we cannot even begin to predict. The struggles Vallabhbhai faces, the obstacles he overcomes—those are what shape him into the leader he will become. He is meant to walk this path, and we must not interfere."*

The children exchanged uneasy glances.

Subhas, his voice small but determined, spoke up, *"But we just want to help him finish his work so he can play."*

Revanth's gaze softened. He sighed, his fingers gently tracing the Kālachakra Kāda on his wrist, as if contemplating something deep within himself.

"I know your intentions are good," he said softly. *"And in most cases, my answer would be no. But…"*

He glanced back at Vallabhbhai, who was returning to his work.

"This is different," he finally said, more to himself than to them.

Siya, unable to contain her curiosity, asked, *"What do you mean?"*

Revanth's eyes flickered with something distant, as if he were looking through time itself. *"There are moments in history that must remain untouched. But then, there are moments… where a small kindness doesn't change history—it strengthens it."*

Ajay came forward, still trying to grasp what Revanth was saying. *"So… it won't change anything?"*

Revanth nodded, his voice steady, as if offering them a sliver of truth. *"Vallabhbhai Patel is destined to become the Iron Man of India. He would rise, no matter what. Whether or not you give him a pencil or help him for a few minutes—it will not alter his path. If anything, it may offer him a small moment of ease before he returns to his duty."*

He placed a reassuring hand on Ajay's shoulder. *"Help him. But remember, the journey is his, not yours to change."*

The children nodded slowly, understanding the gravity of what he was saying.

Siya turned back to Vallabhbhai, her gaze softening as she watched him pause for a moment, rubbing his forehead, the charcoal smudging across his skin.

"Alright," she said softly. *"Let's help him."*

With a shared look, the children approached Vallabhbhai. He looked up at them, surprised but composed. *"Are you looking for someone?"* he asked, setting his charcoal aside.

Siya smiled warmly. *"We're just travellers. We've been walking through the village and saw you working. We thought you might like some help."*

Vallabhbhai studied them for a beat, his gaze thoughtful before shaking his head gently, a polite but firm smile playing on his lips. *"Thank you, but this is my family's work. I must do it myself."*

Vishwa, noticing the rough, uneven paper Vallabhbhai was working with, ran his fingers lightly over the frayed edges, his eyes softening. His hand instinctively reached for the small notebook and pencil tucked in his bag.

Subhas and Dharani exchanged a quiet, knowing glance before reaching into their bags, each pulling out their own supplies.

"We weren't offering to help with the work," Dharani said gently, her tone calming,*" but maybe this would help with your studies?"*

Vishwa, nodding in agreement, gently pushed the notebook and pencil toward Vallabhbhai. Dharani and Subhas quickly followed suit, offering their materials as well.

Vallabhbhai's face softened in quiet curiosity as he examined the smooth, clean pages. His fingers traced the edges, marvelling at the paper's texture—so different from the rough, uneven sheets he was used to.

"I've never seen something like this," he admitted softly, his voice tinged with quite surprise.

For a brief moment, his eyes held something unspoken—a blend of gratitude and quiet longing.

"But why would you give this to me?" Vallabhbhai asked, his gaze shifting from one child to the next. *"You don't even know who I am."*

Siya met his gaze, her voice soft. *"Don't worry about that. We have more than enough supplies. It looks like you're studying hard to become something more than a farmer. We just thought we could help."*

Vallabhbhai took the notebooks and pencils with a cautious yet sincere nod. *"Thank you,"* he said, his voice low. *"I hope to become a lawyer one day."* He paused, then asked, *"But who are you, really?"*

Vishwa, unable to contain his excitement, spoke up. *"We're students too. We're traveling with our uncle, and…"*

"*Well, we travel and learn about different places, people and cultures.*" Siya finished his sentence, knowing that they couldn't reveal anything.

Vallabhbhai smiled faintly. "*That sounds interesting. I'd love to travel and learn, but here...*" He gestured to the fields. "*There's work to be done. I don't have time for anything else.*"

Siya, recognizing the weight of his words, hesitated before asking, "*Do you ever get time to play, Vallabh?*"

Vallabhbhai paused, caught off guard for a moment. His expression flickered between surprise and caution.

"*How did you know my name?*" he asked, his voice soft with curiosity.

The children exchanged uneasy glances, each of them unsure how to answer.

Ajay, thinking quickly, shrugged. "*We heard someone mention it earlier, around the village.*"

Vallabhbhai studied them for a moment before nodding thoughtfully. "*Ah, I see. Well... not always.*"

His expression softened, but a hint of sadness lingered in his eyes.

"*I love to play—kabaddi and gilli-danda, especially. But there's no time for that. I have to study or work.*"

He gestured toward the fields stretching behind him. *"There's always work to be done."*

After a brief pause, Vallabhbhai turned back to them, his curiosity piqued. *"What are your names, by the way?"*

Vishwa stepped forward eagerly. *"I'm Vishwa, this is my sister Siya, and—"*

One by one, he introduced the rest of the group, each child offering a polite nod and a warm smile.

Sarojini, her voice soft and kind, said, *"What if we helped you finish your work faster? Then you could take a little time to play."*

Vallabhbhai appeared surprised. *"You don't need to do that."*

Ajay stepped forward, grinning. *"Come on Vallabh, just for a little while. We'll help with the fieldwork, and then you can show us how to play these games. We've never played these games before."*

Vallabhbhai hesitated for a moment, glancing between them and the field. Then, finally, a flicker of curiosity sparked in his eyes.

"I suppose... but only if we finish the work first," he said, a reluctant smile tugging at the corners of his lips.

The children sprang into action, eager to help.

But ploughing a field proved to be much harder than they anticipated.

Ajay struggled to push the plough, his feet slipping on the uneven ground, as the thick soil stubbornly resisted his every move. Dharani tried to lead the oxen, but they barely budged under her guidance, the animals seeming almost indifferent to her commands.

"How does he do this every day?" Ajay panted, wiping the sweat from his brow, clearly exhausted.

Vishwa and Subhas, their determination fuelling their efforts, grabbed the plough with renewed vigour while Vallabhbhai patiently guided them. With a few strained efforts and a lot of sweat, they finally managed to carve a neat furrow through the soil.

"Nice!" Vallabhbhai nodded, clearly impressed by their persistence. *"You're getting the hang of it."*

One by one, the children took turns, working alongside Vallabhbhai. With each passing minute, their respect for the labour he did every single day grew.

Even Revanth, standing at a distance, watched them with quiet approval. His smile never wavered.

Finally, with the fieldwork completed, Vallabhbhai looked around, his eyes lingering on the children. Vishwa, still buzzing with excitement, clapped him on the shoulder. *"Now it's your turn, Vallabh! Teach us one of your games."*

Vallabhbhai wiped his hands on his kurta, the dust and sweat from the fieldwork still clinging to him. Despite his exhaustion, his expression softened as he gestured toward a small clearing nearby.

"Alright. It's my turn now, I suppose," he said with a grin. *"I'll teach you how to play gilli-danda."*

Vishwa's eyes lit up with enthusiasm. *"Yes! This is going to be awesome!"*

Vallabhbhai grabbed a small wooden peg (gilli) and a longer stick (danda). With practiced ease, he balanced the gilli on a rock, then swung the danda, sending the peg soaring through the air before it landed far away.

"That was incredible!" Subhas shouted, his eyes wide with amazement.

One by one, the children took turns trying to hit the gilli. Sarojini, Dharani, and Siya missed completely, Subhas and Vishwa knocked it only a few feet away. After three tries, Ajay finally sent it flying, much to everyone's delight.

The clearing echoed with laughter as they took turns, enjoying the simplicity of the game. For a brief moment, Vallabhbhai was just a child again—playing freely, unburdened by the weight of responsibility and the future that awaited him.

Revanth, standing at a distance, blinked away a tear, deeply moved by the scene unfolding before him.

As the sun sank lower, casting long shadows across the fields, he finally stepped forward. His voice, gentle yet firm, cut through the laughter like a soft breeze.

"It's time to move forward."

The children, still smiling from the game, turned to Vallabhbhai. He looked back at them, reluctant to part ways, his expression reflecting a quiet sadness at the impending goodbye.

"Thank you," he said softly, his voice heavy with gratitude. *"For the notebook, and... for this."*

His eyes glistened with unshed tears, and for a moment, words failed him. He couldn't quite find the right way to express his gratitude for their kindness.

"We should be the ones thanking you, Vallabh." Siya replied with sincerity. *"We've learned so much from you today."*

Vallabhbhai chuckled softly, his gaze lingering on each of them, as if memorizing their faces.

"I'm glad. Maybe, one day, our paths will cross again."

Revanth placed a reassuring hand on Vishwa's shoulder, gently guiding the children back toward the path.

"Come," he said warmly. *"There is more to see."*

They waved goodbye to Vallabhbhai, and as they walked away, he returned to his spot beneath the tree, the notebook and pencil still in his hand. He traced the smooth pages again, his thoughts already returning to his studies.

The sounds of their laughter slowly faded into the evening air, but something about this encounter lingered with Vallabhbhai—like the whisper of a future yet to unfold.

Chapter 12

A Father's Moment of Healing

The golden glow of the setting sunbathed Nadiad's fields as the children walked in silence. The village behind them had already begun to fade into history, yet something about it clung to them—like the feeling of waking from a dream too vivid to forget.

Vishwa, usually the first to break the silence, shuffled his feet and glanced at the others. *"Do you think he'll ever remember us?"* he asked, his voice softer than usual.

Ajay, staring at the ground, sighed. *"He barely knew us. We were just travellers passing through."*

"But we gave him his first notebook," Dharani pointed out. *"What if that moment actually mattered to him?"*

Siya nodded thoughtfully. *"Even if he forgets our faces, maybe, just maybe, he'll remember that someone once believed in him."*

Revanth, who had been listening quietly, finally spoke. His voice was warm but edged with something unreadable. *"True, sometimes the smallest kindness leaves the deepest mark."*

He paused, then turned toward them with a knowing look. *"But tell me… how did it feel? To not just read history, but to step inside it?"*

The children exchanged glances, struggling to put their emotions into words. Finally, Ajay, of all people, was the first to answer.

"It's different," he said, hesitating. *"When we learn history in school, it's just names and dates. But today, I feel like I actually know him—not as the 'Iron Man of India' but as Vallabhbhai, the boy who worked hard, studied with limited resources, and barely had time to play."*

Dharani clutched her sketchbook tightly. *"I want to remember all of this. Not just as a story but as something real."* She had already managed a couple of pencil sketches during their first journey.

Revanth studied them with quiet approval. *"Good. That means you're ready for the next step."*

Siya glanced at him, eyes full of anticipation. *"Where are we going next?"*

Revanth's eyes gleamed with excitement. *"To the other side of the world. It's time for you to see how Vallabhbhai Patel went from a humble farmer's son to one of the finest barristers, having studied in England."*

With a wave of his hand, a shimmering door appeared, glowing with the colours of dawn. *"This time, we travel to London."*

The portal shifted and shimmered, its golden glow fading into hues of grey and blue. As the children stepped through, the air changed abruptly.

The warmth of Gujarat vanished, replaced by the crisp bite of cold air.

Tall buildings lined the streets, a stark contrast to the sprawling fields and simplicity of rural India.

The moment their feet touched the ground, they shivered. The sky was overcast, thick with fog, and the scent of damp stone and coal smoke lingered in the air.

Sarojini wrapped her arms around herself. *"It's so cold here,"* she whispered. *"Nothing like home."*

Standing beside her, Revanth exhaled sharply, his breath visible in the frigid air, eyes widening in realization.

"Ah, I may have overlooked something."

Ajay's eyes flicked toward Revanth. *"What now?"*

Revanth gave them an apologetic grin. *"Your clothes. They don't exactly blend in."*

The children glanced down at themselves. They looked completely out of place in their traditional Indian attire, their bare arms covered in goosebumps from the cold.

"Oh great," Ajay muttered, rubbing his arms. *"I suppose we're supposed to walk around London like this?"*

Revanth chuckled. "*Of course not.*"

He snapped his fingers.

A soft golden glow flickered around them, shimmering like morning frost melting under the sun.

Within seconds, their clothes shifted and transformed.

Ajay gasped as his kurta morphed into a crisp woollen coat over a buttoned shirt and trousers, polished leather shoes replacing his sandals.

Siya and Dharani now wore elegant long skirts with fitted blouses and woollen coats, their scarves wrapping snugly around their necks. Their hairstyles had subtly shifted, now styled appropriately for the era.

Vishwa and Subhas found themselves clad in knee-length coats, breeches, and polished boots, their usual casual energy momentarily forgotten as they marvelled at their transformation.

Sarojini hugged her now-warm coat close, her eyes wide. "*That... that was incredible.*"

"*I have my ways,*" Revanth said with a wink, adjusting his own long overcoat.

Ajay pulled at his stiff collar. "*You couldn't have given us something more comfortable?*"

"*Fashion comes with a price, my friend,*" Revanth teased.

Siya twirled once, admiring her coat and gloves. *"Alright, I have to to admit—this is kind of amazing."*

Revanth smirked. *"Now that you won't freeze to death, let's continue. This is where Vallabhbhai Patel's journey brought him next—far from Nadiad, far from everything he knew."*

The streets bustled with people—men in formal suits and hats, women in heavy coats, and horse-drawn carriages clattering over wet cobblestones. Gas lamps flickered dimly through the mist, casting a soft, golden glow on the stone buildings.

Subhas stared at the towering buildings in amazement. *"It's so different here; everything feels bigger, faster."*

Revanth smiled. *"London, 1910. This is where Vallabhbhai arrived to study at Middle Temple, one of the most prestigious legal institutions. But the grandeur of this city was no comfort to him. He had left his home, his family, and everything familiar behind."*

Then, suddenly, as if the mist parted just for them, a grand structure emerged—Middle Temple.

Its stone walls loomed ahead, proud and imposing, its arched windows catching the faint light of the evening lamps.

The children's steps slowed as they took in the building's magnificence.

Middle Temple stood tall before them, its weathered stone walls exuding age-old wisdom and discipline. Ornate carvings lined the archways, and stained-glass windows glowed faintly under the overcast sky.

Yet, it wasn't the grandeur that caught their attention.

On the broad stone steps, a lone figure sat hunched over a thick book.

Vallabhbhai Patel.

But he was no longer the boy they had met in Nadiad.

He was now a man.

His posture was straight but weary, and he scanned the pages with dark, intent eyes. His once carefree expression was now one of quiet intensity, as knowledge and duty began to weigh heavily on him. Dressed in a simple but well-kept suit, he looked like someone who belonged here—yet something in his expression suggested he felt like a stranger.

Heavy law books and notes, some marked with hastily scribbled annotations, were scattered around him.

As the children observed him, they noticed something deeper.

With a subtle shift in his expression, his sigh heavy with weariness.

This was not mere tiredness; there was something heavier in that sigh. Beneath the surface lingered a sadness, like a storm waiting to break.

Subhas pointed. *"Is that him? He looks different."*

Revanth, standing beside them, nodded. *"This is Vallabhbhai Patel, several years older than when you last met him. The boy who balanced work and study in Nadiad is now a man, facing new challenges."*

Ajay frowned, arms crossed. *"He looks sad. It's more than just the studying, isn't it?"*

Siya tilted her head, picking up the same feeling. *"No, it seems deeper. What could have happened in these years?"*

Revanth, standing behind them, sighed softly. *"Yes, much has changed. The Vallabh you knew has faced many challenges since those days in Nadiad."*

He gestured toward a nearby bench, its dark wood damp from the misty air. The children gathered around him, their curiosity laced with quiet concern.

Revanth settled onto the bench, looking toward Patel, whose fingers lightly traced the edges of his book—his mind clearly elsewhere.

Then, finally, Revanth began.

"After you met Vallabhbhai in his childhood, his life took many paths," he said, his voice steady yet low. *"He*

married a woman named Jhaverba, and together they had two children—Maniben and Dahyabhai. They were a happy family, but as his responsibilities grew, so did the pressure of his obligations. He worked hard, balancing his duties as a husband, father, and lawyer."

Leaning forward, Dharani whispered, *"So he was still working toward becoming a lawyer?"*

Revanth nodded. *"Yes, his determination never wavered. He aspired to rise beyond a farmer's life, serving his people in greater ways, working relentlessly and saving for something more."*

But then, Revanth's voice softened, as if his words were heavy with unspoken meaning.

"But in 1909, tragedy struck."

The children leaned in, the cold air forgotten.

"Suddenly, his wife Jhaverba fell ill and passed away."

The group fell into a stunned silence.

Sarojini covered her mouth, eyes welling up. *"He lost his wife?"* she whispered.

"Yes," Revanth said solemnly. *"It was unexpected, leaving him with two young children to care for. Devastated, yet aware he couldn't fall apart, he knew his children needed him."*

The impact of his words resonated deeply within each of them.

Vallabhbhai, still seated on the temple steps, turned a page in his book, his expression unreadable.

Siya's throat tightened. *"And what did he do?"*

"He made the hardest decision of his life," Revanth continued. *"He left."*

Dharani blinked, confused. *"Left? But… why?"*

"Because he had a dream," Revanth explained, *"a dream that could no longer wait. Entrusting his children to the care of his family, he set off for England to pursue his studies at Middle Temple in 1910—not only to learn, but also to escape the weight of his grief, hoping distance would aid his healing."*

Ajay swallowed hard, his gaze fixed on the man they had once seen as a boy.

"He didn't just leave home," Ajay murmured, *"he left everything he loved."*

Revanth nodded. *"And yet, he never stopped moving forward."*

The group remained silent, the fog swirling gently around them.

Subhas was the first to find his voice.

"It makes sense now," he murmured, *"he's not just worried about his studies—he's carrying so much more."*

Vallabhbhai, still seated on the steps, turned a page in his book without urgency. He was so consumed by his thoughts that reading had become a difficult task.

"Yes," Revanth replied softly. *"But it hasn't been easy. Every step towards success pulls him further from his family, and the grief never leaves. He feels the weight of his responsibility—both as a father and as a man who will help shape the future of India."*

The children's gazes remained fixed on Patel.

The world around him thrived—carriages rattled past, men hurried by with umbrellas and briefcases, the distant hum of conversation filling the air—yet he seemed untouched by it all.

A man alone in a city full of people.

Ajay exhaled slowly, his usual sarcasm nowhere to be found. *"He looks so alone."*

Revanth placed a reassuring hand on Ajay's shoulder. His voice was gentle, but firm.

"He is, but this is his path to walk. We cannot interfere."

The words hung in the air.

But something shifted in Sarojini.

She wasn't looking at Patel as a historical figure anymore. She wasn't thinking of him as the man who would one day be called the *Iron Man of India.*

She saw him as a father—then she saw her father in him.

A father who had left behind his daughter.

Her throat tightened.

Maniben must have missed him so much. Did she understand why he left? Did she cry for him at night, as I would if my father were gone?

The thought gripped her heart like a vice.

The more she stared at Patel—his solitude, his quiet sorrow—the more unbearable it became.

She took a step forward.

"Sarojini—" Siya's whisper of warning barely reached her ears.

Revanth's voice sharpened. *"Wait. You cannot—"*

But Sarojini couldn't stop herself.

Her feet moved before her mind could catch up, and before she knew it, she had stepped away from the group.

Ignoring the others, she approached Vallabhbhai.

Vallabhbhai didn't notice her at first.

His world had shrunk to nothing but the endless pages of law books and the heavy silence of loneliness. The cold stone steps beneath him were as unyielding as the grief that burdened his heart.

But then—

A small presence beside him.

For a moment, he thought it was a memory.

A faint shadow of someone who used to sit beside him, before she was too far away to do so.

He blinked.

She was real.

A little girl—not his Maniben, but somehow just like her.

Her dark eyes, deep with understanding beyond her years, studied him with quiet patience. She didn't speak right away. She just sat there, her presence soft and steady, as if she had all the time in the world.

"Are you alright?" her voice barely above a whisper.

Vallabhbhai inhaled sharply.

It had been so long since someone had asked him that.

Too long.

He let out a slow breath, rubbing his forehead.

"I'm fine," he murmured.

The words felt wrong the moment he spoke them.

The truth sat just beneath them, heavy and suffocating.

"There's just... a lot on my mind."

He forced a smile, but it was weak—like paper stretched too thin over something about to break.

Sarojini didn't push.

She didn't probe or press for more.

She sat there, letting the silence breathe between them.

The distant clang of carriage wheels, the muffled voices of strangers, the cold, damp air of London—they all faded into the background.

After a long moment, she spoke again.

"You look tired," she said gently.

"Like you've been carrying something heavy for a long time."

Vallabhbhai stilled.

The words struck deep, touching something he had buried beneath responsibilities, ambition, and the quiet, aching loneliness of being a father so far from home.

Turning fully toward her, his tired gaze searched her face.

And then, it happened.

For a split second, the fog of time blurred, past and present merging into one.

He didn't see Sarojini.

He saw Maniben.

His daughter.

Sitting on the floor beside him as he read, patiently waiting for him to finish so she could tell him about her day.

The same wide, knowing eyes.

The same quiet strength.

"You remind me of my daughter," he whispered, words slipping out before he could stop them.

His voice shook.

He hadn't spoken of her to anyone here.

"She's back in India. About your age."

Sarojini glanced up at him, but she didn't react with surprise.

She understood.

In that same moment, she didn't see Vallabhbhai Patel.

She saw her father.

How he sat at the hospital late into the night, exhausted yet persevering.

His soft sighs when he thought no one listened.

The quiet sacrifices.

She saw her father in Vallabhbhai's tired eyes.

And it hurt.

Vallabhbhai let out a shuddering breath, his fingers tightening around the edges of his law book.

"It's been so long since I've seen her or my son."

His voice was barely there, just a breath carried away by the wind.

"I came here to build a better life for them, but some days I wonder if I made the right choice—leaving them behind after their mother passed."

A deep, aching silence.

The words hung between them, unspoken but heavy.

And at that moment, Sarojini couldn't take it.

The thought of Maniben, sitting at home, waiting for a father who wasn't coming back anytime soon—aching for him the way Sarojini knew she would if she were in her place—was overwhelming.

She swallowed hard.

Instinctively, she reached for her taaviz—a simple thread her father had tied around her wrist before she left for this school trip.

"It will keep you safe," her father had promised.

She closed her fingers around it.

Then she carefully slipped it off.

"Here," she said softly.

Vallabhbhai looked down.

In her open palm rested the taaviz—a simple piece of thread with a tiny charm, worn from time and love.

"My father gave this to me," she whispered, *"it's supposed to protect me, but maybe... it could help you too."*

Vallabhbhai stared.

For a moment, he found himself back home.

Maniben's small hands tying a Rakhi on Dahyabhai's wrist.

The sound of his children's laughter filling their house.

The warmth of a home he hadn't seen for a long time.

His vision blurred.

His first instinct was to refuse.

"You should keep it, child," he began, but the look in her eyes—so full of sincerity, so reminiscent of his daughter's—stopped him.

Slowly, hesitantly, he allowed her to tie the taaviz around his wrist.

It was a small thing.

A thread.

A gesture.

Yet, it broke him.

His emotional dam shattered.

Vallabhbhai closed his eyes, his face contorting, as a single tear traced down his cheek.

Sarojini didn't hesitate.

She wrapped her arms around him, embracing him as if he were her own father.

And for the first time in years, Vallabhbhai Patel—the strong, unyielding man the world would one day know as the Iron Man of India—allowed himself to be vulnerable.

He released a shuddering breath, his arms coming up to embrace her, his fingers gripping her shoulder as if holding onto something he had lost.

Tears slipped down both their faces.

Neither uttered another word.

But in that silence, something healed.

For the first time in a long while, Vallabhbhai Patel was more than just a Barrister.

He was a father.

And for Sarojini, for that single moment—

He was hers.

From afar, the other children watched, their eyes wide with a mix of surprise and understanding.

Even Revanth, who had cautioned against interference, stood in silence.

Because he saw it.

Sarojini's small act of compassion wasn't changing history—it was simply offering comfort to a man who needed it.

Revanth's gaze softened.

"Sometimes," he murmured, more to himself than to the others, *"a reminder of what one is fighting for is all that's needed."*

As the hug ended, Patel sat back, exhaling shakily, his fingers brushing over the taaviz now tied to his wrist.

For a long moment, he just held it, as if absorbing the warmth left behind in the thread.

Then, slowly, he smiled.

It was subtle, barely noticeable at first—but genuine.

A tentative flicker of light after a long storm.

He turned toward Sarojini, his voice steadier now.

"Thank you," he said, his words carrying more weight than she realized. *"I needed that more than you know."*

Sarojini smiled, her heart swelling.

"You'll be okay," she said kindly. *"Your children miss you, but they understand you're doing this for them. And when you return, they won't just be proud—they'll know they had the strongest father in the world."*

Vallabhbhai's fingers tightened slightly around the taaviz, grounding himself in those words.

He saw Sarojini walk away, and for the first time in what felt like forever, the faces of Maniben and Dahyabhai didn't feel like memories drifting away.

They felt closer.

He reached for his law books, lifting them—feeling not the strain of duty, but the strength of his conviction.

The journey was still long.

But now, he felt he could walk it again.

From a distance, Revanth observed the scene quietly.

His gaze rested on Sarojini, watching the small but powerful exchange.

As she walked back toward him and the other children, she said, *"I'm sorry. I couldn't bear seeing him like that."*

No one spoke back.

Revanth finally responded.

"You've done well," he said softly, admiration filling his voice.

"Even small acts of kindness can lift the heaviest burdens. But now, it's time to leave Vallabhbhai to his journey."

Sarojini hesitated.

She glanced back.

Vallabhbhai was still sitting there—his fingers absently tracing the taaviz, lost in thought.

But he wasn't hunched anymore.

He stood taller.

Just before she turned away, she saw him watching her too.

Their eyes met in a brief, quiet moment.

A moment where neither spoke, but both understood.

And then she turned back to Revanth and the others, and they started walking away.

As the children disappeared into the mist, Vallabhbhai raised his wrist, fingers brushing over the thread. The cold London air bit at his skin, but the warmth of the taaviz remained—like a distant echo of home.

Then, the fog parted.

A familiar shimmer appeared: a glowing portal, swirling with the colours of dawn, poised to take them to their next destination.

Revanth gestured toward it; his voice gentle yet firm.

"Come," he urged, his words resonating with a depth beyond mere instruction. *"The journey is far from over."*

Chapter 13

....

The Heart of Resistance

The swirling colours of the portal faded, and the familiar glow of their previous journey dimmed. The children stood still, enveloped by the pulsating energy of Revanth's portal space. The air around them hummed softly, the remnants of time itself shifting and settling.

Revanth spoke with a calm but firm voice. *"Before we move forward,"* he began, *"I want you to understand where we're going next."*

The children gathered closer; their curiosity evident.

"You've seen Vallabhbhai as a boy, determined to study and improve his life, and again in London, grappling with loss and duty. But time has passed," Revanth explained, his gaze flickering with something unreadable. *"He returned to India as a barrister, a successful lawyer. Yet, something within him had changed. He had seen the injustices faced by his people and knew he couldn't simply practice law. He had to fight for their rights."*

Dharani responded, considering his words. *"So, he went from being a lawyer to what? A leader?"*

Revanth nodded. *"Yes. A leader of people who had no voice. He witnessed the struggles of farmers—ordinary men and women—being taxed by the British despite enduring years of drought. The Kheda Satyagraha was one of his first acts of leadership, where he organized a peaceful resistance against these unjust taxes. It was here that he became Sardar Patel, a leader for the poor and the oppressed."*

Ajay's brow furrowed. *"But how can you fight without fighting?"*

"Through unity and nonviolence," Revanth explained. *"Inspired by Gandhiji, Patel ji led farmers in peaceful protest. They refused to pay taxes—not out of defiance, but out of necessity. Their strength was not in weapons, but in their unwavering resolve. And in the end, their unity forced the British to listen."*

The children nodded, understanding the gravity of what they were about to witness.

"Now," Revanth said, motioning toward the swirling portal before them. *"It's time for you to see how Patel ji stood with the people of Kheda and led them through one of their darkest times."*

With a wave of his hand, the portal shimmered and shifted, revealing a vast, sun-scorched land. The moment the children stepped through, a dry, suffocating heat enveloped them. The air was thick with dust, and the scent of parched earth and burning straw lingered like an unspoken warning.

The land stretched before them, cracked and lifeless. What had once been fields of grain now lay barren, the soil split into deep fissures from the relentless drought. The trees, sparse and brittle, stood like silent witnesses to the suffering of the people.

A heavy stillness hung in the air, broken only by the distant murmur of voices: the tired, strained whispers of farmers who had run out of hope.

Vishwa wiped sweat from his forehead, his voice barely above a whisper. *"It's like everything here is dying."*

Subhas shivered, not from the heat. *"It feels empty,"* he murmured. *"Like even the air has given up."*

Revanth's expression darkened. *"This is Kheda, Gujarat, in 1918. The farmers here have endured years of drought. Their crops have failed, and they have nothing left. Yet, the British government still demands heavy taxes. If unpaid, their lands and homes will be seized."*

Vishwa's eyes widened. *"How are they supposed to pay if they have nothing?"*

Revanth sighed. *"They can't and that's why they are desperate. Many have sold their belongings just to survive. Some have abandoned their homes while others are simply waiting, too weak to fight back."*

In the distance, under a large banyan tree, a group of farmers stood, their faces etched with exhaustion and desperation.

Vallabhbhai Patel.

Now a little older, he was no longer the young man they had seen in London. His face, weathered by time and struggle, carried the marks of numerous hardships. Yet his presence was unshaken, like a storm-weathered rock standing firm against crashing waves.

He listened intently to the village elders speaking, arms crossed, his expression deep in thought. Unlike the others, his eyes were not filled with despair, but determination.

"We cannot pay the taxes, Patel ji," one of the farmers said, his voice cracking with exhaustion. *"Our fields are dry; we have nothing left. If we lose our land, we lose everything."*

Patel remained silent for a moment, his gaze sweeping over the villagers. When he spoke, his voice was calm but unyielding.

"Then we will not pay."

A hush fell over the crowd.

"But Patel ji, if we refuse, the British will come for us. They will take our land, our cattle, our homes."

Patel's expression remained unwavering. *"Let them try."*

Murmurs spread through the group. Some of the farmers exchanged uncertain glances, while others nodded, as if they had been waiting for someone to give them the strength to stand.

The children, watching from a distance, could feel the shift in the air.

The significance of this moment surpassed anything they had ever experienced—not just a man fighting against injustice, but an entire community on the brink of something greater than themselves.

And yet, even as Patel reassured the villagers, there were others who were still suffering.

Siya's gaze shifted beyond the gathered men to a shaded spot beneath the banyan tree.

Children—small, frail figures huddled together, their faces gaunt with hunger. Some clung to their mothers; others sat in silence, their eyes hollow and empty.

A little girl whimpered softly, *"We haven't eaten in days. I'm so hungry."*

Siya's breath caught in her throat; Dharani stiffened beside her.

The other children had noticed, too.

Ajay clenched his fists. "*This isn't fair,*" he muttered. "*It isn't just about taxes—these people are starving.*"

Subhas swallowed hard. "*We have to help them,*" he whispered, his voice trembling.

Revanth turned toward them, his face unreadable. "*I know what you're thinking,*" he said quietly. "*But remember what I told you—history must not be changed.*"

Siya, still staring at the crying children, whispered, "*But how can we stand by and do nothing?*"

For a long moment, Revanth didn't respond.

Then, softly, he said, "*That is the very question Patel ji asked himself.*"

For a long moment, the children stood in silence, watching the suffering unfold before them. The weight of history pressed against their hearts—this wasn't just a moment in time; it was a battle for survival.

Ajay's gaze flickered between the crying children and Patel ji, whose firm stance before the farmers embodied resilience, but not immediate relief. They could not change history, but they could ease suffering—if only for a moment.

Without another word, he moved, noticing Subhas doing the same.

They quickly gathered the little food they had in their bags—a few pieces of bread, some fruit, and a handful of biscuits. It wasn't much, but it was something. The other children followed suit.

Ajay knelt beside the smallest girl, whose frail frame was shaking from hunger, and gently placed a piece of bread and some biscuits in her tiny hands.

"*Here, eat this,*" he said softly, his usual sharpness replaced by an unfamiliar kindness.

The girl hesitated, staring at the food as if unsure whether it was real, then she took it cautiously with trembling fingers. Tears still clung to her lashes, but for the first time, her expression softened.

"*Thank you,*" she whispered.

One by one, the children distributed whatever they could spare, offering quiet words of comfort. The food would not change their fate, but for a brief moment, it eased their suffering.

From a short distance, Patel watched.

At first, he was merely observing—a habit formed from years of leadership. Yet something about these young strangers struck a chord deep within him. They were not from this village. They were not farmers' children. And yet, they were here, kneeling beside the poorest of the poor, offering what little they had.

His gaze drifted to the farmers' children, their small hands clutching the food as if it might disappear. Their eyes held more than just hunger—they held a kind of knowing, a silent acceptance of struggle far beyond their years.

The sight touched something raw inside him. This was why he fought—not for power, not for politics, but for the simplest of things: food, dignity, a chance at childhood.

"These children should not be here," Patel thought, feeling a weight press against his chest.

"They should be playing, learning—not knowing hunger like this."

A memory flickered into life.

A hot afternoon. A dusty field. Six children helping him finish his chores, pulling him away from duty and into the simple joy of a game. The sound of their laughter, the freedom of running barefoot across the earth, the feeling of being a boy—not a worker, not a student, just a boy.

His fingers instinctively reached for his wrist.

There, worn yet unbroken, the taaviz still clung.

For years, he had kept it without question. He did not know the face of the one who had tied it around his wrist, nor could he remember her name. But the gesture—the warmth of small hands, the strength in a single embrace—had never left him.

It was strange, the way such moments lingered. A single act of kindness, carried through time like a whisper.

He exhaled slowly and turned back to the gathered farmers.

They formed a semicircle before him, their bodies tired but their hearts determined. They had lost so much, yet still, they stood.

Patel straightened his back, his voice steady as he prepared to speak.

It was time to remind them that they were not powerless.

He stepped forward, his presence both commanding and calm. As he spoke, the murmurs in the crowd faded into silence, his voice carrying across the parched fields.

"Brothers and sisters," he began, his words steady but filled with unwavering resolve. *"We do not stand here today to raise our fists in anger, nor to fight with weapons. We stand because this land—our land—is not just soil beneath our feet. It is our home, our lifeline. And it belongs to us, not to those who tax us without mercy."*

A hush settled over the villagers as his words sank in.

"We refuse to pay not out of defiance, but out of necessity. We cannot give what we do not have." His voice rang with certainty, his conviction unshaken. *"But hear me well: we will not bend; we will not cower. If we allow fear to divide us or give in to despair, they will win. Yet, if we*

stand together, firm in our resolve—peaceful, patient, and unbreakable—no power in this world can defeat us."

His gaze moved across the weary faces before him, taking in the farmers, the mothers, the hungry children clinging to their fathers' legs. He met their eyes, one by one, giving strength where there was doubt.

"Our battle is not against men," Patel ji continued. *"It is against injustice. And injustice cannot withstand unity. It will crumble before those who refuse to surrender."*

A ripple of quiet determination moved through the crowd. Some villagers nodded, others clenched their hands at their sides, not in anger, but in quiet solidarity.

"Stay firm." Patel ji's voice softened, yet it lost none of its power. *"Stay peaceful. Stand with one another. And we will win."*

The air around them charged with the electric atmosphere of witnessing a pivotal moment in history. The children stood motionless, their hearts pounding as the sheer magnitude of Patel ji's words pressed into their souls.

Ajay swallowed hard, his earlier skepticism forgotten. Dharani gripped her bag's strap, her fingers tightening as though trying to hold onto the moment. Siya, her eyes fixed on Patel ji, felt something shift deep inside her—a realization of what true leadership meant.

But before they could absorb more, a warm hand rested gently on Sarojini's shoulder.

"*It's time to go,*" Revanth murmured, his voice tinged with a quiet finality.

Sarojini blinked, torn from Patel ji's speech. "*But he's just begun,*" Ajay whispered, reluctant to leave.

They watched the villagers cheer Patel ji's words, with someone shouting, "*We will stand together!*"

Revanth smiled—a knowing, almost bittersweet smile. "*There are moments you are meant to witness and others you must leave behind. You have seen enough to understand the power of Patel ji's words. His leadership will carry them forward. But now, we must move on.*"

Reluctance flickered in their expressions, but they understood. Slowly, they turned away, their footsteps light against the dusty ground as they followed Revanth.

As they walked, Patel's voice echoed behind them—his unwavering conviction filling the air like a promise. A reminder of the power of peaceful resistance. Of courage. Of unity.

As they stepped into the unknown, they carried his words with them.

Chapter 14

Bardoli: The Birth of Sardar

The golden hues of the Kheda landscape faded behind them as the children entered the pulsing energy of Revanth's portal. The echoes of Patel ji's words, the hunger in the farmers' eyes, and the strength of their wordless defiance still clung to them.

The air around them shimmered softly, and Revanth let them stand in silence, absorbing what they had witnessed.

Then, finally, he spoke.

"What you witnessed in Kheda was Patel ji's first step into leadership," he began. *"But he was not alone. Gandhiji led the movement, guiding Patel ji and the farmers toward nonviolent resistance."*

Siya frowned thoughtfully. *"So, Kheda wasn't entirely his own fight?"*

Revanth nodded. *"Exactly. It was his initiation—a test of his resolve, his ability to stand with the people. But the next time he took on the British, it was different. The stakes were higher. The fight was his own."*

Ajay leaned forward, intrigued. "*What do you mean? What happened next?*"

"*Bardoli,*" Revanth announced, his voice filled with gravity.

The air crackled with anticipation as Revanth continued. "*Ten years after Kheda, Patel ji was no longer just a supporter of a movement—he was its leader. When the British imposed an unfair tax hike on the farmers of Bardoli, there was no Gandhiji by his side. This time, it was Patel ji who stood alone at the frontlines, guiding the people, carrying the weight of their hopes and struggles on his shoulders. For the first time, it was not just a fight for justice—it was a fight that rested entirely on him.*"

A hush fell over the group.

Clutching her sketchbook, Dharani said, "*So… this time, he wasn't just learning to lead. He was leading.*"

Revanth's lips curled into a knowing smile. "*Yes.*"

With a sweeping motion of his hand, the portal swirled, shifting colours, morphing into a dusty path lined with vast fields.

As the portal settled around them, the children felt the world shift. The humid air of Kheda was replaced by something different—a strange mix of tension and determination hanging in the very air of Bardoli.

They stepped onto a dusty road where the sun cast long shadows across the land. Vast fields stretched into the distance, golden and green, but there was no sense of peace here. The land looked ripe with harvest, yet the faces of the people were etched with worry.

The village square was packed with farmers and their families, their expressions a mixture of frustration and desperation. Women clutched their children, eyes darting toward the crowd's edges, as if expecting trouble. Men stood in clusters, whispering with fists clenched and backs straight.

There was anger here, but not the reckless kind. It was a simmering storm, held back only by the voice of one man standing at the centre of it all.

Vallabhbhai Patel.

He stood on a raised platform, his white dhoti crisp, his shawl draped over his shoulder as he addressed the people. There was no hesitation in his stance, no fear in his voice.

"We will not bow," Patel declared, his voice resounding over the murmuring crowd. *"They can demand, they can threaten, but they cannot shake the ground we stand on. This is our land. Our sweat has nurtured it, our hands have tilled it, and we will not surrender it to injustice."*

A murmur of agreement swept through the crowd, laced with uncertainty.

A farmer stepped forward—his face sunburnt, his clothes worn from toil. His voice shook as he spoke.

"But Patel ji, how much longer can we hold out?" he asked, his eyes darting around as though afraid of being heard. *"The British have sent notice after notice. They will come. And when they do… they will take our homes, our fields, our cattle. What will we do then?"*

A ripple of fear passed through the villagers.

Another man added, *"Some of us have already lost everything. We cannot pay with what we do not have. But what if they punish us? What if they throw us in prison, or worse—"* His voice dropped, *"Use force?"*

A wave of unease settled over the crowd, their voices rising in anxious murmurs.

Mothers tightened their grip on their children. The men exchanged uneasy glances.

Then—

A sharp voice sliced through the thick tension of the crowd.

"We will not just stand here and suffer!"

A group of young farmers surged forward, their faces dark with anger. Their hands gripped sticks, wooden staffs, and even curved sickles—the very tools they used to plough their land now held with the intent to strike.

"If the British try to take our homes, we will fight back," one of them shouted.

Another man slammed his stick into the dust, fury locking his jaw. *"We are not weak, Patel ji! If they come with force, we will give them force in return!"*

Anger spread through the crowd like wildfire.

A few more raised their voices in agreement, lifting whatever weapons they had. The tension thickened as rage, fuelled by years of oppression, threatened to boil over.

Siya gasped, her heart hammering.

This was no longer just fear; it was the brink of something dangerous.

If they struck back, the British would have the excuse they needed to crush them.

She looked to Patel ji, her pulse racing.

Would he tell them to fight?

Would he let them choose war?

Patel ji raised a single hand—silent, commanding.

The effect was instantaneous.

The crowd stilled, their anger hanging in the air like a storm ready to break.

Patel took a step forward, his voice cutting through the rising heat of their emotions.

"No."

One word.

Firm. Final. Unshakable.

The men with sticks hesitated.

Patel ji's eyes burned with certainty as he faced them, unafraid.

"You lift your weapons out of anger. I know that anger— I carry it too."

He paused, letting his words settle.

Then, his voice dropped lower, filled with unmistakable power.

"But consider this—if we resort to violence, we abandon the principles that define our struggle. Our true strength lies not in causing harm, but in our unwavering commitment to truth and justice."

The men gripping their sticks hesitated.

Patel ji's eyes softened with empathy as he continued.

"Violence feeds more violence, birthing a cycle of hatred and ruin. Only by choosing nonviolence do we stand unbroken, exposing injustice without surrendering our humanity."

A silence fell over the village. His words left a profound impression.

The men holding weapons lowered their arms slightly, uncertainty flickering in their eyes.

Patel stepped forward once more, his very presence a fusion of command and compassion.

"Our aim is not to defeat the British through bloodshed but to awaken their conscience—and the world's—to the righteousness of our cause. Through peaceful resistance, we demonstrate our inner strength and resolve."

His eyes sought the young farmer who had spoken first.

"Will you join me on this path of nonviolence? Will you place your trust in the strength of our unity and the justice of our cause?"

The young man looked down, his grip on the stick loosening.

"I... I never thought of it that way, Patel ji."

Patel nodded, a gentle smile forming.

"Remember: true courage lies not in raising arms, but in possessing the patience and fortitude to endure suffering for a greater good."

Gradually, one by one, the farmers lowered their weapons, the fire in their eyes giving way to steely determination.

Patel ji addressed the crowd, his voice imbued with hope.

"Together, through nonviolent resistance, we will show the world the strength of our character and the righteousness of our cause. Let us be firm, let us be resolute, but let us also be peaceful."

A murmur of agreement spread through the villagers.

The moment had passed.

The storm had calmed.

And the path had been set.

They would fight. But they would fight Patel ji's way.

They would fight without violence.

But with unwavering strength of unity.

The air in Bardoli had stilled, charged with a tension that amplified every heartbeat. The crowd of farmers, once drowning in uncertainty, now stood united behind Patel ji, their backs straight, their hands clenched—not in anger, but in resolve.

Then—the sound of marching boots.

Distant at first, but unmistakable.

Siya felt it before she saw them—the sheer force of approaching authority, the unmistakable presence of an oppressor who had always ruled with force.

The ground beneath them vibrated as rows upon rows of British soldiers appeared at the edge of the village. Their pristine, pressed uniforms stood in stark contrast to the farmers' simple attire. Their boots clattered against the dry ground, their polished rifles slung across their shoulders like silent threats.

They were not here to negotiate; they were here to conquer.

The villagers stiffened, gripping each other's hands, whispering quiet prayers under their breath.

Siya's stomach clenched—they looked ready for war.

At the front, a British officer mounted on a black horse wore a uniform heavier with badges than the others. His gaze was cold and calculating. Behind him, a tall, lean officer stepped forward, his mustache twitching with thinly veiled irritation as he scanned the crowd.

Finally, the lead officer dismounted and advanced with slow, deliberate steps.

His voice, thick with condescension, slashed through the strained silence.

"I see your stubbornness remains intact, Patel."

Vallabhbhai Patel, his hands clasped behind his back, did not flinch.

His voice, unlike the officer's, was calm, measured, and immovable. "*We have made our decision, Sir. The people of Bardoli will not pay.*"

The officer's lips curled in irritation. "*This is blatant insubordination,*" he barked. He turned to the gathered villagers, addressing them instead. "*Your leader here thinks he can protect you. But tell me this—how will he save you when we take your homes? When we seize your land? When we leave you with nothing but dust beneath your feet?*"

A ripple of nervous murmurs spread through the crowd.

The other officer, the tall, lean one, stepped forward. His expression was sharper, crueller.

"*This is your last chance: comply and pay what you owe.*"

When no one moved, his eyes flickered with annoyance.

Then, he turned to Patel ji.

His stance shifted, silently escalating the tension. His fingers twitched, as if resisting the urge to draw his baton. He moved closer to Patel ji, his voice dropping to a dangerous whisper.

"*If you think this is a game, Patel—you are gravely mistaken.*"

His words slithered into the air, a quiet threat.

Then, deliberately taking slow steps, the officer raised his hand, as though preparing to strike.

And that's when it happened.

A flash of movement.

A blur—motion and instinct fused together.

Siya moved—pure reaction, pure heart.

She leaped forward, sprinting through the crowd with arms outstretched, placing herself directly between Patel ji and the British officer.

Her chest heaved with adrenaline, her arms spread wide, like a living shield.

Her voice cut through the air, sharp and fierce. "*STOP!*"

Everything frozearound her.

The officer stared at her, his hand still hovering mid-air, his eyes wide with shock.

The crowd gasped, their murmurs turning into stunned silence.

Even Patel ji blinked, momentarily caught off guard.

Siya's breath was unsteady, but her stance was firm. She was just a child—yet she stood against an empire.

The British officer's confusion turnedinto disbelief—and then amusement.

"Step aside, girl," he sneered, *"this is not your fight."*

But Siya stood her ground. Her small frame did not shrink, her hands did not drop.

"If you want to touch him, you'll have to get through me first."

She only knew one thing—Patel ji could not fall.

There was a shift in the air.

And then—

Patel ji's gaze found hers. For a moment, the world held its breath.

Then, slowly, he smiled.

Not a smile of amusement.

Not a smile of reassurance.

A smile of understanding.

And with a voice calm, unshaken, timeless, he said—

"Let them take our lands, child; they will never take our courage."

Siya's lips parted in awe.

Something swelled in her chest; a realization, a moment of clarity.

And before she even realized what she was doing—

She spoke—loud, clear, unshakable.

"*Sardar.*"

The crowd stilled.

Then—

The name caught and spread like wildfire.

A whisper. "*Sardar.*"

A murmur. "*Sardar.*"

A roar. "*SARDAR!*"

The voices grew. The ground itself seemed to tremble.

"*SARDAR! SARDAR! SARDAR!*"

The British officers stiffened, hands twitching as they sensed a force far beyond their control rising.

Patel ji stood there, silent, listening. His face revealed nothing. But deep in his eyes, something shifted.

Not pride.

Not ego.

Just purpose.

And he nodded.

Not in acceptance. But in acknowledgment.

The people had made their choice.

A leader had been named.

The children barely remembered leaving Bardoli. One moment, they were lost in the roar of "*Sardar*"— the next, they were somewhere else. The next, they found themselves back in Revanth's portal, the air still humming with the power of what they'd seen.

Ajay spun towardsher, eyes wide. "*That was—*"

Before he could finish, Revanth's voice cut through.

"*Reckless,*" he said, his tone sharper than usual—laced with frustration and concern. "*You could have been seriously hurt.*"

Siya, still catching her breath, turned to him with a small, knowing smile. "*But I wasn't.*"

Revanth didn't look amused. If anything, his expression darkened.

But Siya wasn't finished. She met his gaze, unwavering. "*Besides… I trusted you.*"

A flicker of emotion crossed Revanth's face—too quick to name.

"*You promised you'd keep us safe, didn't you?*"

For a moment, there was silence.

Ajay and the others exchanged glances, waiting for Revanth's reaction.

And then—he let out a heavy sigh.

A long, slow breath, as if debating whether to scold her or admit he was impressed.

Finally, shaking his head, he muttered, "*You have little regard for my rules, don't you?*"

But a faint smile betrayed him, tugging at the corner of his mouth.

A moment of quiet settled between them, but it didn't last long.

Subhas, still buzzing with curiosity, turned to Revanth. "*What happened after that?*"

Revanth exhaled, the intensity of the moment easing into something softer. "*The British backed off.*"

The children exchanged glances, stunned.

"*Just like that?*" Ajay said, eyebrows raised in disbelief.

Revanth smirked. "*Not immediately, but they soon saw what Patel ji had established in Bardoli—a wall of unshakable resistance. The farmers refused to pay, leave, or break. Without their cooperation, the British had no power.*"

Still reeling, Siya murmured, *"So they gave in."*

Revanth nodded. *"Yes. They reduced the taxes. The farmers got their lands back. And Patel ji… became more than just a leader—he became a symbol of strength."*

"The newspapers carried his story everywhere. His victory in Bardoli echoed in every corner of India. And among those who heard of it, was Gandhiji."

The children straightened immediately, their interest piqued.

Ajay leaned forward. *"So what happened when he heard it?"*

With amusement flickering in his eyes, Revanth crossed his arms. *"What do you think happened? Want to storm into one of Gandhiji's meetings, introduce yourselves, and ask him?"*

The group froze, exchanging wide-eyed glances.

Ajay grinned, his eyes gleaming. *"You mean we can?"*

Revanth shot him a look. *"No, Ajay."*

Dharani sighed. *"You shouldn't have put it that way—now he actually wants to."*

Ajay shrugged, unapologetic. *"Just checking."*

Revanth shook his head, a chuckle escaping before he continued. *"You don't always need to crash into history. Sometimes, a peek is enough."*

Siya shot him a questioning look. "*A peek?*"

Revanth snapped his fingers, and right beside them, a small, rectangular glow appeared in the air. It flickered before solidifying into what looked like…

Vishwa frowned. "*…a window?*"

Revanth spread his arms grandly. "*Behold—the Window of Time.*"

The children stared at the glowing frame.

Subhas blinked. "*That looks like just a normal window.*"

Ajay squinted at it. "*Not even a particularly impressive one.*"

Revanth sighed dramatically. "*Look, not every moment in time needs a grand portal. Sometimes, a simple window will do.*"

Dharani crossed her arms. "*Is this some kind of clumsy time travel joke?*"

Revanth grinned. "*Obviously.*"

Ajay grinned back. "*I respect that.*"

Revanth rolled his eyes. "*Can we focus?*"

With an exaggerated wave of his hand, the glowing window shimmered, revealing another time and place to the children.

In a simple room lined with books, cushions, and a spinning wheel, Mahatma Gandhi sat cross-legged across from Vallabhbhai Patel.

The children leaned closer, wide-eyed.

Gandhiji's voice, calm yet warm, filled the room. *"You did well, Vallabh. Bardoli stood strong because of you."*

Patel, ever modest, shook his head. *"Bardoli stood strong because of its people."*

Gandhiji smiled, his eyes gleaming. *"And who stood with them, if not you?"*

Patel said nothing, but the quiet determination in his eyes spoke volumes.

Then, a thoughtful expression crossed Gandhiji's face. He tilted his head slightly, as if weighing something in his mind.

"Tell me, Vallabh, am I also supposed to call you by your new name now?"

Patel blinked, clearly confused. *"New name?"*

Gandhiji's smile broadened.

"Sardar."

The children quietly gasped, watching as Patel stilled.

Gandhiji, observing Patel's reaction, spoke softly. *"This is not just a title, Vallabh. It is something you have earned."*

For a moment, Patel remained silent. Then, with quiet acceptance, he inclined his head.

The conversation continued, as if nothing extraordinary had happened. But the children knew better.

Siya turned back to the window, watching as Gandhiji and Patel continued their discussion, the name already embedding itself in history, becoming something greater than a title—an identity.

Sardar Vallabhbhai Patel.

As the conversation faded, Revanth snapped the window shut, sealing the moment in time once again.

He turned to the children with a small smile. *"Shall we continue?"*

Chapter 15

....

The Iron Will:
Patel's Stand for Unity

The portal's soft glow faded leaving Revanth and the children once again in the tranquil space that had become their familiar haven. The gravity of what they had witnessed—Patel ji's leadership, his defence of farmers, his unshakable faith in nonviolence—still clung to their minds.

The children listened intently as Revanth paused, his eyes shifting toward the swirling portal behind them. *"The next chapter in his life was even more challenging. It wasn't just about freeing the farmers or standing up to the British."*

"In 1947, after generations of struggle, the dream of millions of Indians came true. On August 15, 1947, India won her freedom."

Siya's eyes brightened at the mention of that fateful date. *"We read about that in school! It was such a huge victory. But... they didn't talk much about Patel ji."*

Revanth nodded, his gaze thoughtful. *"That's true. Many know about the fight for independence, about leaders like Mahatma Gandhi and Jawaharlal Nehru, but not everyone understood that Patel ji's work was far from over on that day. Many celebrate the fight for freedom, but few realize that Patel ji's hardest work began after that day."*

Ajay, always drawn to the toughest battles, leaned forward. *"What do you mean? What was left to do?"*

Revanth's voice deepened. *"Winning freedom was one thing. But Patel ji had to ensure that India remained united after independence."*

The children frowned. *"United?"*

Revanth nodded. *"Yes, India had won her freedom—but not her unity. At that time, it comprised over 500 princely states, each ruled by kings, nawabs, and maharajas. Not all of them wanted to join India."*

Subhas' face scrunched up in confusion. *"But why wouldn't they want to be part of India?"*

Revanth sighed, his voice steady as he explained. *"You have to understand—these rulers had absolute power over their lands for generations. Becoming part of India meant giving up their control. Some feared losing their wealth, their armies, and their independence. Others... were tempted by different offers."*

A puzzled look crossed Siya's face. *"Wait. You're saying Patel ji had to convince all 500 of them?"*

Revanth nodded. "*Exactly. And not all of them were easy to persuade.*"

The air around them grew heavier as he continued. "*He employed diplomacy and persuasion, and when necessary, firm resolve.*"

His tone deepened as he spoke the next words. "*Consider Junagadh, for instance. The Nawab opted for Pakistan, despite the majority of his people desiring to be part of India.*"

Ajay clenched his fists. "*That's not fair!*"

"*It wasn't,*" Revanth agreed. "*So Patel ji took strategic action. He deployed forces not to attack, but to restore order. Ultimately, the people of Junagadh were given a choice, and they overwhelmingly chose India.*"

The children exchanged glances, grasping the enormity of Patel ji's responsibility.

A brief silence followed.

Then, Siya spoke the words they were all thinking.

"*And Hyderabad?*"

Revanth's expression darkened slightly. He let out a slow breath. "*That was the most challenging of them all.*"

The air around them felt heavier as Revanth continued.

"The Nizam of Hyderabad was one of the wealthiest rulers in the country. He had an army of his own, alliances he was trying to build, and a firm belief that Hyderabad should remain independent. But his people—millions of them—wanted to join India."

Siya's brows knitted in concern. *"So Patel ji needed to convince him, just like he did with the others, right?"*

Revanth exhaled slowly. *"He tried. Patel ji prioritized diplomacy, offering the Nizam every chance to join willingly. However, the Nizam refused to cooperate, stalling negotiations in hopes of outside help—perhaps even from Pakistan. Hyderabad's independence would be more than a political issue; it would threaten everything Patel ji had fought for."*

A tense silence stretched between them. The realization settled in.

"So what did Patel ji do?" Ajay asked, his voice quieter than usual.

Revanth's expression was unreadable, but his voice was steady. *"He took decisive action, marking a pivotal turn in history."*

He took a step forward, and with a graceful motion of his hand, the door in the portal shimmered open before them.

Inside, the swirling colours—gold, deep crimson, and burning amber—appeared to resonate with the depth of history. There was something different about this portal. The energy felt… heavier.

The children stared at the shimmering doorway, a mixture of curiosity and unease in their eyes.

Revanth turned back to them, his gaze calm but firm.

"Come," he said. *"Witness one of Patel ji's greatest victories, not merely in words but through action—first in the halls of diplomacy, then on his own battlefield."*

The children exchanged glances, then took a deep breath.

Before they could step through, Revanth raised a hand. *"Wait,"* he said.

The children halted mid-step, glancing at him in confusion.

"There's a crucial step we must take before we proceed," he said, his eyes twinkling.

Vishwa, always the most excitable, leaned forward eagerly. *"Another portal trick?"*

Revanth's lips quirked. *"Something like that. But this time, it's not about blending in—it's about not being seen at all."* He let the words settle before adding, *"We need to be invisible!"*

For a moment, silence.

Then—

"*Invisible?!*" Vishwa exclaimed, practically bouncing in place. "*That's amazing!*"

Ajay's eyes widened. "*Wait—like, actually invisible?*"

Siya folded her arms, ever the skeptic. "*Are you saying you can just... make us disappear?*"

Subhas and Sarojini exchanged glances, equally fascinated yet unsure. "*Is that even possible?*"

Revanth chuckled, his amusement evident. "*In the world of time travel, many things are possible.*" He exhaled lightly, his expression shifting to something more serious. "*But this is more than just a trick, children. We must exercise extreme caution now. We have interfered before—intentionally or not—but this moment in history... I cannot allow that. Not here. Not in Hyderabad.*"

His words stilled them. The excitement in the air faded slightly as they recognized the gravity of the situation.

"*This is different,*" Revanth continued. "*We are walking into a city on the brink of something irreversible. The balance is fragile. We cannot be seen, cannot be heard. We must observe, not interfere.*"

A soft golden light flickered at his fingertips as he lifted his hand. With a slow, fluid motion, he flicked his wrist, sending shimmering mist swirling around them.

It flowed like liquid sunlight, enveloping their forms and blurring their outlines until—

"*Whoa—look at this!*" Ajay whispered, watching his own hand dissolve into thin air.

Vishwa wiggled his fingers, grinning as they vanished. "*I am officially a ghost.*"

Siya, still half-skeptical, exhaled slowly as she looked down—her feet already dissolving into mist. "*I can't believe this is actually happening...*" A reluctant smile tugged at her lips.

"*Don't worry,*" Revanth reassured them, his voice steady. "*This is merely a temporary spell. We'll remain unseen and unheard by outsiders, yet we'll be able to see each other clearly if we want to.*"

Their visible forms completely dissolved into the golden mist.

All that remained were their breaths, hushed whispers, and the quiet hum of the portal behind them.

Revanth nodded, satisfied. "*Now, we are ready.*"

With that, they stepped through the portal, invisible and brimming with anticipation for what awaited them at the heart of history.

The children stood at the far end of the grand hall, their invisible forms pressed close together. Even though no one could see them, they instinctively held their breath, sensing the enormity of the historical event unfolding.

The Nizam of Hyderabad sat at the head of a long, ornate table. The wealth of his kingdom was evident in his surroundings: rich silk drapes, golden plates and spoons, intricate chandeliers, and polished marble floors reflecting the flickering candlelight. His robes, adorned with precious gems, shimmered under the dim glow—a silent testament to his unmatched power.

And yet, power alone did not dictate fate.

At the other end of the hall stood Sardar Vallabhbhai Patel.

He wore no silk, no gold, no jewels—only the crisp simplicity of a white dhoti, kurta and a shawl. His stance was composed, his face impassive—but his eyes held something far greater than wealth: unshakable resolve.

A standoff.

The air itself seemed to tighten around them.

Patel spoke first. *"Your Highness,"* his voice was firm, unwavering. *"Hyderabad is not merely a piece of land on the map; it is an integral part of India—its people, its culture, its history. The time has come for us to stand united, not as separate entities, but as one nation. I urge you to reconsider and join the Union peacefully."*

The Nizam's fingers drummed against the polished wood of the table, slow and deliberate. His dark eyes studied Patel, calculating.

"I have made my position clear, Sardar Patel, not once but several times. Hyderabad will remain independent. I see no reason to relinquish my sovereignty or the power I hold over my people."

A tense silence followed.

Patel stepped forward slightly, his hands still folded behind his back, his voice carrying an edge of finality.

"This concerns not only your power, Your Highness, but also your people. The vast majority of Hyderabad wants to be part of India. You have ruled with authority, but now, it is time to rule with wisdom."

The Nizam scoffed and leaned back in his chair, the candlelight flickering across his sharp gaze.

"My people are loyal to me, and their desires are irrelevant if they conflict with my decision. Hyderabad is prosperous; we have no need for your Union."

The children, standing in their invisible forms, watched in stunned silence.

Ajay clenched his fists. *"He's really going to refuse?"*

Patel maintained his unyielding posture, but his voice took on a darker tone.

"This is not only about what you need. India cannot be divided, piece by piece. The time for fragmented kingdoms is over. We are forging a future greater than ourselves—and it must come before personal power."

The Nizam's grip tightened on the armrest of his golden chair. His irritation was growing.

"You speak of unity, yet I hear only coercion. Should you seek to intimidate me, Sardar, know that Hyderabad stands ready to defend itself."

The room felt colder.

The children stiffened. Dharani's instincts kicked in. "This… this feels like it could lead to a fight."

Patel's face remained unreadable, but his voice grew softer—dangerously so.

"I seek no conflict, Your Highness, yet India stands prepared to defend its integrity. While we have offered friendship, Hyderabad cannot remain an isolated island within our nation. Should you refuse to unite, we must act."

The Nizam's fingers stilled against the wood.

For the first time, his face betrayed something beyond arrogance—hesitation.

He knew Patel's words were not empty.

Hyderabad stood proud, but it stood alone.

And alone… it was vulnerable.

His voice, now quieter but still icy, barely concealed the war raging inside him.

"And what will the history books say, Patel?" he asked, his lips curling into a sneer. *"That Hyderabad was forced into submission? That I surrendered to avoid war?"*

Patel exhaled sharply, a faint trace of sadness flickering in his eyes.

But resolve eclipsed regret.

"The history books will say," he murmured, *"that Hyderabad, under your leadership, stood with its people, recognizing that unity is strength."*

A pause.

A breath.

"Or," Patel continued, his gaze never unwavering, *"they will note that Hyderabad was brought into the fold through force, solely due to your decisions. The choice, Your Highness, is yours."*

A heavy silence swallowed the room.

The children barely dared to breathe.

The Nizam met Patel's steady gaze—his expression unreadable, his resolve unyielding.

The weight of an empire, of hundreds of years of rule, of pride and power, all clashed in that single moment.

A decision loomed.

A breaking point.

Revanth, sensing the shift in the air, gently placed a hand on Subhas's shoulder, his voice barely above a whisper. *"Let's give them their space."*

The children, still caught in the gravity of the moment, turned reluctantly.

With one final glance at the two men standing on the brink of history, they reluctantly followed Revanth out of the hall.

As they walked away, the tension from the meeting still clung to them. The children found themselves back in the soft glow of the portal space, the transition between history and their present moment.

Silence stretched between them, heavier than before.

The golden mist that had cloaked them shimmered softly, fading away. One by one, their forms became visible again—yet none of them spoke immediately.

Each was lost in deep thought.

The gravity of what they had just witnessed pressed against their minds. This wasn't like Kheda. This wasn't Bardoli. There had been no fiery speeches that rallied people to stand up against injustice. No peaceful defiance.

This… felt different.

Finally, Vishwa was the first to speak. His voice, usually full of excitement, was quieter now. *"Revanth, what happens now? Will the Nizam give in?"*

Revanth turned to the group, his expression steady, but serious.

"Patel ji hoped for a peaceful solution," he said. *"Yet the Nizam remained firm in his refusal. When diplomacy fails, history often resorts to action. That is when Patel ji had to make a difficult choice."*

He paused before continuing.

"That's when he authorized Operation Polo."

The children exchanged glances, the unfamiliar name hanging in the air.

Subhas's eyes widened. *"What's Operation Polo?"*

Revanth's gaze darkened slightly, his voice careful, measured. *"It was a swift military operation carried out by the Indian Army in September 1948,"* he explained. *"With the Nizam refusing to join India and Hyderabad's private militia, the Razakars, were stirring unrest. If left unchecked, the situation could spiral into something far worse. Patel ji knew India could not afford that risk."*

Siya frowned, struggling with the thought.

"But... Patel ji was a man of peace, not conflict. We saw his commitment to peace in Kheda and Bardoli."

Revanth inclined his head. "You're right. Patel ji always sought peace first. He was never one to choose violence. But he also understood that peace must be protected."

The words settled over them like a slow realization.

"Operation Polo was not waged for conquest, but to preserve unity before chaos could break India apart. Patel ji understood that a protracted conflict would ultimately harm the people more than anything else. So he acted swiftly. The operation lasted only five days. And in the end, the Nizam surrendered."

Finally, Dharani, her eyes narrowed in thought. spoke.

"So, Patel ji had to deploy the army to keep India united?"

Revanth nodded. *"Yes. It was not an easy decision, but it was a necessary one."*

The children exchanged glances, understanding dawning over them.

For the first time, they saw leadership in a new light.

Leadership wasn't merely about words, grand speeches, or inspiring moments.

Sometimes, leadership meant making impossible choices.

In a quiet voice filled with admiration, Siya whispered, *"He was like a shield for India, keeping everything from breaking apart."*

A gentle smile flickered across Revanth's face. *"Precisely. He earned the title '**Iron Man of India**' not through battles fought, but through his unbreakable will to hold the country together."*

The children remained silent, absorbing this new side of Patel ji—the **Iron Man of India**, not just a leader of peaceful protests, but a leader who knew when to act decisively to protect the unity of the nation.

The ensuing silence was unlike the previous one; it wasn't heavy.

It was thoughtful. Respectful.

A newfound understanding of Patel ji had settled within them.

Finally, Sarojini spoke, her gentle words carrying a firm certainty. *"He fought not merely with words or the army; he fought with his heart. His battle wasn't solely against the Nizam—it was for India."*

Revanth's eyes gleamed with quiet pride. He nodded.

"Exactly, Sarojini. Patel ji dedicated his all—not for power, not for personal gain, but for the people of this land. He fought to build a nation that could stand strong,

united, and free. And because of him..." Revanth's gaze lingered on each of them.

"India stayed whole."

....

Chapter 16

Through Legacy and Love: A Leader's Embrace, For One Last Time

Once again, the children stood in the swirling portal, their minds heavy with all they had witnessed. They had met one of the greatest figures in history, witnessed pivotal moments, and had been shaped by the lessons of leadership, unity, and resilience. Revanth was looking around, preparing to open another door.

But this time, the atmosphere felt different—quieter, more solemn. There was no rush or urgency, only an almost sacred stillness. Beside them, Revanth stood, his eyes reflecting a quiet knowing.

As they prepared to step through the portal, he looked at the children, his voice softer than usual.

"There's one more visit to make," he said, his voice soft yet laden with a sense of significance the children couldn't fully grasp.

Siya tilted her head, curiosity in her eyes. *"What are we witnessing now? Do we have to be invisible again?"*

Revanth smiled slightly. *"Sardar Patel ji again. But this time, it's not for you to witness a historical moment. Not invisible. Today, you get to meet him just as yourselves, and yes—visible to him. I think it's time for you to thank him."*

The children exchanged glances, excitement flickering in their expressions. This time, they were more than silent observers. They would engage with him—not as anonymous figures from history, but as their true selves.

The door opened, bathing a quiet room in soft golden light, with the warm hues of the setting sun stretching across the wooden floor. The air smelled faintly of parchment and old books, of stillness and thought. A cool breeze stirred the curtains at the window, where, seated in peaceful solitude, was Sardar Vallabhbhai Patel.

He gazed out over the landscape, his frame still strong yet his presence calmer, as if for the first time in his life, he had nothing left to fight. His hands rested gently in his lap, his face thoughtful.

Revanth gestured for the children to step forward. *"Go ahead,"* he said softly, *"introduce yourselves."*

Siya swallowed hard, stepping forward cautiously. *"Sardar Patel ji?"* she called out, her voice tinged with reverence.

At the sound of her voice, Patel turned. His gaze met theirs, warm yet puzzled. His sharp eyes studied them for a moment, kind but searching.

"I'm sorry, children, but... have we met before?"

The children hesitated, unsure how to respond. Siya stepped forward cautiously, her voice soft. *"Yes, Patel ji... we've met you several times. You taught us so much about leadership and unity."*

But Patel only looked at her kindly, a faint crease of confusion on his face. He shook his head slowly. *"I... I don't seem to remember."*

The children exchanged glances, their joy at seeing him again tempered by the realization that he did not recognize them.

Revanth stepped forward, his voice calm and reassuring. *"Patel ji, these children are no ordinary visitors. You've met them before—on your journey through time. Perhaps the burdens of this life have dimmed that memory."*

Patel's brow furrowed even more, trying to grasp at something just beyond his reach. Revanth then raised a hand, his movements slow and deliberate, and said, *"Perhaps this will help."* As he chanted softly, a golden light began to shimmer around them, filling the room with a soft, warm glow. The light enveloped Patel gently, and for a brief moment, it seemed as though time itself had slowed.

As the golden light gradually receded, a transformation swept across Patel's face. His eyes, which moments ago held uncertainty, suddenly widened with recognition.

His gaze softened, his breath caught, and a new warmth radiated across his features. The memories surged forward, unstoppable—like a river breaking through a dam. Each moment, each lesson, came rushing back, intertwining with the understanding of how Revanth had guided the children through his life, across time itself.

A soft chuckle escaped him, his voice trembling with emotion. *"Ah, yes, yes, now I remember. I remember you all."* A wave of emotion surged through him as he wiped at his eyes, his smile broadening with the sheer joy of reunion. *"I never thought I'd see you again, my dear friends."*

The children beamed, their hearts overflowing with joy upon seeing the love and warmth in Patel ji's eyes.

Siya, overwhelmed with gratitude, was the first to speak. *"Thank you, Patel ji. You showed me that leadership means uniting people—even when it's difficult. I won't forget that."*

Dharani followed, her voice quiet yet deeply heartfelt. *"You showed me that strength isn't just in power, but in finding peace and unity. You protected India by keeping it whole."*

Ajay stepped forward, his tone solemn. *"You taught me that sometimes, the right decision is the hardest one. I'll* remember that, and I'll try to make the right choices, even when it's tough."

Vishwa, ever enthusiastic, grinned at Patel ji. *"No matter what stood in your way, you never gave up. You always stood strong. I want to be that strong, too!"*

Patel ji's heart swelled with pride, his eyes brimming with joyful tears as he listened to the children. But there was more to come.

Finally, Sarojini and Subhas stepped forward, their voices soft but sincere.

Sarojini, her eyes filled with admiration, spoke first. *"I learned that kindness and small actions can make a big difference. You've taught me to care for others, just like you cared for India."*

Subhas, standing a little shyly beside her, added, *"And you taught me that unity is important—when people come together, they can do amazing things."*

Patel ji's eyes softened even more. He didn't respond to each child individually, but his gaze swept across them all with profound affection. His voice, quiet yet deeply emotional, conveyed his feelings. *"I'm glad,"* he said, his voice trembling slightly. *"I'm really glad I could help you learn so much. You've all made my day—more than you know."*

His eyes lingered on Sarojini, and a tear slipped down his cheek. He pulled out the age old taaviz from his desk drawer. "*Sarojini,*" he said softly, "*may I ask for one more hug? The comfort it gave me last time in London... I will never forget it.*"

A lump formed in Sarojini's throat. She stepped forward without hesitation, her arms wrapping around Patel just as she had done before.

Patel ji's arms enfolded her, firm yet gentle. The embrace held a weight beyond words—a moment of pure connection, across time.

For a brief moment, the world around them stood peaceful and still.

Then, without a word, the rest of the children joined in, surrounding Patel ji in a warm embrace. It wasn't just a hug—it was a moment of gratitude, of love, of unspoken admiration for the man who had taught them so much. They held him tightly, not fully understanding the depth of this moment, but feeling the weight of their emotions in their hearts.

Patel ji closed his eyes, allowing the warmth of the embrace to fill his soul. His heart swelled with peace as tears of happiness streamed down his face. He had spent a lifetime fighting for unity, for the people of his nation, and now, in these final moments, he felt something even greater—a love that would outlive him.

Tears also stung the children's eyes, mirroring Patel ji's deep emotions.

From the side, Revanth watched quietly, a gentle smile on his face. Patel ji met his gaze, their eyes locking in a silent communion of understanding. *"Thank you,"* Patel ji's eyes seemed to say. *"For bringing them to me. For giving me this."*

Revanth gave a single nod, his own heart full.

The moment lingered, heavy with emotion. But, as all moments do, it had to end.

Revanth gently placed a hand on Ajay's shoulder. *"It's time,"* he whispered, his voice barely audible.

The children hesitated, not wanting to step away, but when Patel ji himself nodded at them, silently reassuring them, they knew they had to go. Slowly, reluctantly, they stepped back toward the portal.

As the shimmering light enveloped them and they stepped through, the weight of everything they had just experienced still hadn't settled in.

"There's something I didn't tell you before," Revanth said softly as they stood in the golden space of the portal. His voice carried an unusual heaviness. "This was the last day of Patel ji's life."

Silence.

The words hit like a sudden thunderclap. The children froze.

Sarojini, still feeling the warmth of Patel's embrace, felt her heart drop. "*What?*" she whispered, her voice breaking. "*But he... he never mentioned it... Neither did you.*"

Revanth's gaze was kind, filled with a deep, knowing compassion. "*He didn't need to speak it aloud. He knew, and he was prepared. Your words, your expressions of love—they brought him peace. You reminded him that his legacy will live on. That's why I brought you to him today.*"

Ajay swallowed hard. "*So... we helped him say goodbye.*"

Revanth nodded gently. "*Yes. But remember, Patel ji's life is not one to mourn. His legacy, his work—they live on, in all of you. His life was a victory, a gift to this nation. And now, that gift lives through your actions.*"

The children stood silent, struggling with their emotions.

Vishwa was the first to find his voice, though it quivered with emotion. "*I'll always remember how strong he was. He never backed down, even when things got hard. I'll never forget that.*"

Revanth smiled warmly, but his eyes drifted toward Sarojini.

She stood apart, tears streaming freely down her face. She shook her head, her sobs coming faster now. *"I don't want to say goodbye,"* she whispered. *"He was so kind… He asked me to hug him, he made me feel like I mattered. I can't…"*

Without hesitation, Revanth knelt beside her, his expression compassionate. *"I know, Sarojini. I know it's hard. But remember—what you gave him mattered. The comfort you gave him, the love you showed—that is what he took with him. That is what helped him find peace."*

Sarojini sobbed into her hands, her body trembling. The others stood beside her, silent, sharing her sorrow. The weight of loss pressed against them, heavy and inescapable. And then, in the quiet, Revanth's voice emerged, soft and steady, like a hand guiding them back to the light.

Revanth placed a firm but gentle hand on her shoulder. *"It's okay to cry. He loved you dearly, and you loved him just as much. But Patel ji wouldn't want you to carry this sadness. He would want you to remember the joy, not the pain."*

The other children gathered around her, their own eyes red with tears, but their hearts full of understanding.

Subhas wrapped an arm around her, his own face streaked with emotion. *"We'll never forget him, Sarojini. He'll always be with us, in everything we do."*

Sarojini sniffled, her voice trembling. *"I'll remember how he taught us to be kind and how to care for people, no matter what. I'll never forget that."*

Revanth stood, his face glowing with quiet pride. *"That's right. And by remembering that, you'll carry his legacy forward. He may be gone, but his lessons will stay with you forever."*

The children nodded, their tears still flowing, but a palpable shift occurring within each of them.

Vishwa wiped his face with the back of his hand, managing a small, brave smile. *"He really was the best. He was a real superhero."*

Revanth's eyes sparkled. *"He was indeed. And now, it's your turn to embody his teachings—to stand strong, lead with kindness, and keep India united, just as Patel ji did."*

He exhaled softly, his gaze dropping to the familiar presence of the Kāda on his wrist. He knew it was time.

He raised his wrist, allowing the ancient energy to pulse through him one last time. The air around them stirred, and a final doorway shimmered into existence—the last portal of their journey.

The golden light stretched before them, warm and steady. Siya wiped her eyes and squared her shoulders, her voice quiet but resolute. *"We have to keep moving,"* she declared, locking eyes with the others, determination hardening in her gaze. *"Just like he did."*

The children faced the portal, their grief not erased but transformed. The ache of farewell lingered, yet in its stead, something new took root—a quiet, unshakable resolve.

Chapter 17

A Farewell Bound by Promise

The children felt it deeply—their journey with Revanth was nearing its end. Yet, none were ready to say goodbye.

Revanth, sensing their hesitation, stopped just before they reached the portal that would take them back to their world. The golden glow of the swirling doorway flickered softly, waiting.

He turned to them, his eyes filled with warmth. "*I must leave you now,*" he said quietly. His voice, though gentle, carried a finality that made their hearts ache.

Siya, standing closest to him, swallowed hard. "*But we don't want you to leave,*" she admitted, her voice barely above a whisper.

Revanth's smile was knowing, kind. "*I know,*" he said. "*Never before have strangers felt so much like friends to me. I was glad that I could take this journey with you. I have learned a lot, and I hope you did too.*"

The children nodded, each of them feeling the significance of his words.

"But I have a strong feeling," he continued, his gaze sweeping over them, *"that this isn't really goodbye. I believe we will meet again. Our parting today may lead to other, perhaps even greater, adventures."*

The thought brought a glimmer of hope to their faces.

They didn't want to leave him—after everything they had experienced together, Revanth felt like more than just a guide. He had become a friend.

Vishwa, unable to contain himself, blurted out, *"Can't you stay with us?"*

Revanth chuckled, shaking his head. *"I assure you, this isn't the end. There are more lessons ahead, more journeys for you to take, and I'll be there when the time is right. But for now, you must return to your world."*

Ajay, ever the practical one, frowned slightly. *"But how will we find you again? How will we know you're there?"*

Revanth's lips quirked in amusement. *"Well,"* he said playfully, *"I could give you my visiting card."*

The children giggled, despite the sadness in their hearts.

"But something tells me," Revanth added, his voice deepening into a more meaningful tone, *"you won't need it."*

He reached into the folds of his robe drawing out a small, goldenconch shell that shimmered with an inner glow—the same warm, ethereal light that surrounded their portals. As he placed it in Siya's hands, the glow pulsed gently, as if recognizing her touch.

Revanth closed her fingers gently over it. *"If you ever need me—if your hearts seek answers, or you find yourselves in a moment of true need—this shell will know. Call out for me, and I will hear you, wherever I am."*

Siya stared in awe at the conch shell, feeling its faint warmth radiating through her fingers. Beneath her fingertips, the golden glow flickered softly, the same ethereal light as the portals that had carried them through time.

"Really?" Sarojini whispered, wiping the last of her tears. *"Will you come back if we call?"*

Revanth nodded. *"I will. But only if you truly need me. Trust yourselves, and trust the lessons you've learned. I have faith in all of you."*

Clutching the shell tightly, Siya seemed to anchor herself to the promise it held. She looked up at him, her voice steady despite the lump in her throat. *"We'll take care of it. And we'll look after each other."*

Revanth stood tall, his eyes gleaming with pride. *"I know you will. And I promise—we will meet again."*

Revanth's smile softened as he looked at the children one last time. *"There's something else,"* he said, his voice thoughtful. *"From the moment our paths crossed, I felt a pull—something deeper than fate. Something unfinished. And I still don't know why. I don't fully understand why I was drawn to you all."*

The children exchanged curious glances. Siya, sensing a deeper weight behind his words, tilted her head slightly. *"What do you mean?"*

Revanth's eyes flickered with an unreadable emotion, but he simply shook his head, his smile tinged with knowing. *"That, my young friends, is a mystery I must solve on my own. And when I do..."* He paused, glancing at the golden conch in Siya's hands. *"Perhaps that will be the day we meet again."*

The children smiled through their lingering sadness, comforted by the knowledge that this wasn't truly goodbye. Revanth stepped back, his presence still strong, even as the golden light of the portal began to envelop him. His gaze swept over them one last time, his expression filled with pride.

Then, with a final nod, he dissolved into the mist, merging with the shimmering glow, leaving the children in their bus.

As the bus rumbled through the quiet night, the golden conch lay nestled safely in Siya's hands, its glow gone, its warmth a silent reminder of all they had learned. They all fell asleep one at a time.

The world around them remained unchanged, but they were transformed.

Their journey with Revanth had come to an end, but in their hearts, they knew—somewhere, somehow—it was only the beginning.

Chapter 18

New Beginnings, Everlasting Lessons

The next morning, the children stirred as sunlight streamed through the bus windows. The rhythmic hum of the engine had ceased, now replaced by the distant chatter of their classmates waking up.

For a brief moment, everything felt… normal.

Ajay yawned, stretching his arms. Dharani rubbed her eyes, blinking at the familiar sight of the school trip still in progress. Their classmates, groggy and oblivious, were pulling on their shoes and chatting about breakfast, completely unaware of the night's extraordinary journey through time.

The six of them exchanged glances.

"Was all that even real?"

Siya's heart raced as she reached into her bag. For one terrifying second, she feared it was empty. But then— her fingers brushed against something smooth, cool. She pulled it out just enough for them to see.

The golden conch shell gleamed softly in the morning light, its glow faint yet unmistakable.

Siya smiled, offering silent reassurance. It hadn't been a dream.

The others exhaled, some of them chuckling under their breath.

Ajay smirked. *"So much for waking up in reality."*

As they stepped off the bus, they caught their breath at the breathtaking sight before them.

There, towering into the sky, was the Statue of Unity.

Sardar Vallabhbhai Patel's imposing figure stood proudly over the land, bathed in golden sunlight. His strong features, his unshakable stance—it was the same presence they had come to know on their journey. But this time, it wasn't a historical scene. It wasn't a moment in time.

This was now.

For a moment, none of them spoke.

Dharani's eyes widened. *"It's... different seeing him like this now, isn't it?"*

Subhas nodded, his voice hushed. *"Before, he was a leader in our textbooks. Now... it's as if we truly know him."*

Sarojini inhaled deeply, feeling a lump in her throat. "*We do.*"

Their classmates dashed ahead, eager to explore the museum, while their teachers herded everyone together. But the six of them lingered, reluctant to move on just yet.

Vishwa, hands buried in his pockets, glanced at the others. "*Do we tell anyone?*"

Siya shook her head firmly. "*We can't, remember? Even if we could, no one would believe us.*"

Ajay smirked. "*Yeah, imagine us explaining, 'Hey, we just travelled through time and met Sardar Patel himself!'*"

Vishwa let out a dramatic gasp and clutched his chest. "*Oh no! The time portal is calling us again! Quick, enter it before it disappears!*"

The group burst into laughter, their bond stronger than ever.

This was their story, their secret.

And as they looked up at the towering Statue of Unity, they knew one thing for certain—they would never forget.

As they joined their classmates at the base of the Statue of Unity, their teacher, Ms. Shehnaz, began sharing facts about Sardar Patel's life and legacy.

But the six of them exchanged secretive smiles, having learned far more than any textbook could ever teach.

When she asked questions about Patel's role in uniting India, the six surprised everyone with their profound, insightful responses.

Ajay, always eager to share what he knew, confidently explained Patel's diplomatic efforts with the princely states.

Ms. Shehnaz, clearly impressed, raised an eyebrow. *"That's very detailed, Ajay. Have you all been doing extra reading?"*

Before he could respond, a classmate turned to them, eyes wide. *"How do you guys know all this?"*

Ajay exchanged a glance with his friends, then shrugged casually.

"We did our homework."

Siya, biting her lip to hold back a laugh, leaned toward Dharani and whispered, *"Homework... sure."*

Dharani smirked, shaking her head. If only their classmates knew.

After visiting the statue, the class headed into the Statue of Unity Museum. The halls were lined with exhibits showcasing Patel's life, his role in India's independence, and his fight to unite the country.

For most of their classmates, it was merely another museum trip.

But for the six of them?

It was a journey through memories.

As they navigated the exhibits, they paused before a large black-and-white photograph of Bardoli.

The image captured a moment of history—Sardar Patel, standing firm, surrounded by the people of Bardoli.

Siya froze; she knew this moment—she had been there.

Before she could speak, Dharani nudged her playfully. *"Hey, isn't that the part where you—"*

Siya whipped her head toward her, eyes wide, and whispered urgently, *"Shhh!"*

Dharani smirked. *"I was just saying—it's a great photo."*

Ajay, catching on, grinned. *"Oh, I don't know, Dharani… I think you were about to say something important."*

Siya groaned and covered her face with her hands as the others stifled their laughter.

Despite her embarrassment, she felt a surge of pride and warmth as she gazed at the image.

Turning back to the photo, she gently brushed the glass with her fingers, as if the moment reached out to her across time.

Now smiling more fondly, Dharani spoke in a softer tone, "*Jokes aside—that was really brave, Siya.*"

Siya let out a slow breath, nodding. "*He was the brave one. We just got to stand beside him.*"

The museum visit flew by, a blend of laughter, learning, and quiet reflection.

Soon, it was time to return home.

As the bus rumbled toward the airport, the six friends sat together, gazing out the window, their minds lingering on all they had experienced.

The journey felt surreal, as if time had stretched and compressed around them.

Before they knew it, the plane had taken off, the vast landscapes below shrinking into patches of green and brown. The flight back to Bangalore passed in a blur, a fleeting moment between the past and the present.

For their classmates, the trip was merely another school outing; for them, it was a memory etched in history.

When the bus arrived at their school, students filed off one by one, while the six lingered, sharing silent glances that spoke volumes.

Their journey with Revanth was over.

But the bond they shared?

It would never fade.

"*See you tomorrow?*" Ajay asked, his voice casual yet his eyes revealing more.

Siya nodded, clutching her bag where the golden conch shell lay safely hidden. "*Yeah. Tomorrow.*"

They smiled at each other before stepping off the bus, united by one certainty—some secrets are meant to be kept together.

When the children returned home, the impact of their journey lingered—not as a burden, but as a quiet presence in their hearts.

Siya, ever cautious, carefully locked the golden conch shell inside her small safe, knowing that one day—when the time was right—it would glow and hum again.

Ajay replaced his favourite superhero poster with one of Sardar Patel, a daily reminder that true strength lies not in capes and powers, but in courage, leadership, and responsibility.

Dharani, ever creative, leafed through her sketchbook, each page a vivid recount of their adventures—Patel leading his people, Bardoli, the princely states, even a faint sketch of Revanth in the background, hidden like a secret only she knew.

Subhas sat before his map of India, which had transformed from mere borders and names. Every state and city came alive, brimming with stories to uncover and places to explore. He traced his fingers over the map, dreaming of the journeys yet to come.

Vishwa, overflowing with energy, eagerly shared tales of their trip and Sardar Patel with his family. He omitted the fantastical elements, yet he knew their adventure was far from over.

But for Sarojini, the return home carried a deeper weight.

In her room, she cradled her notebook, the warmth of Patel ji's final embrace still fresh in her memory. He had shown her that even the smallest acts of kindness could change the world—that compassion was as powerful as any great leader's words.

Tears filled her eyes—not of sadness, but gratitude.

She opened her notebook and began to write, her heart steady and her purpose clear.

A simple list.

Ways she could make a difference. Small acts of kindness, just like Sardar Vallabhbhai Patel had taught her.

She smiled softly, gripping the pen a little tighter.

"I'll keep his spirit alive," she whispered. *"By spreading kindness wherever I go."*

Epilogue

A few months had passed since their incredible journey with Revanth and the lessons they learned from Sardar Patel. Life had resumed its normal pace for the six children, though they all carried the memories of their adventure, aware it had transformed them in ways they couldn't fully grasp.

One evening, as the last light faded, Siya sat at her desk, holding the golden conch shell she had faithfully guarded since their return—watching, waiting. Suddenly, the usually dormant conch glowed faintly in her hands and began to hum, as if awakening from a deep slumber. Something was different.

Her phone buzzed on the desk. It was a message from Ajay: "*Hey, do you still have the conch shell? I have this strange feeling something's about to happen. I can hear a humming that no one else seems to hear.*"

Siya's heart raced as she hastily messaged Ajay about the glowing conch shell, urging him to check with the others. Each sensed the same strange energy, feeling as though the air had shifted; they were relieved that Ajay was checking in and that the others felt it too.

Ajay called Siya, who needed to say no more. They agreed to meet at the playground outside Ajay's apartment immediately.

As they convened under the dimming dusk light, the conch in Siya's hand brightened, pulsing in sync with her heartbeat. Vishwa, ever eager, bubbled with excitement. *"Do you think it'll call Revanth if you blow it?"*

Siya scanned the group. *"There's only one way to find out."*

Taking a deep breath, Siya raised the conch to her lips and blew. A deep, resonant sound echoed through the playground, vibrating with ancient power. For a few tense seconds, nothing happened, and the children exchanged uncertain glances.

Suddenly, the air behind them shimmered. They spun around as a familiar portal opened, swirling with gold and silver light spilling from its depths. From within, Revanth stepped out, his eyes sparkling with warmth and mischief.

"You never fail to amaze me," he said, his voice brimming with amusement. *"You figured out how to use the conch shell."*

The children's faces brightened with excitement. Sarojini dashed up to him, her smile wide, and embraced him. *"Revanth! We weren't sure if it would work."*

Revanth chuckled softly, walking toward them. *"Of course, it worked. The conch shell is more than a keepsake; it's a link between us. You called, and I answered."*

The group converged around him, buzzing with questions. But Siya, standing slightly apart, still felt the pull of something she couldn't quite explain. She met Revanth's gaze, and again, she saw that flicker of recognition in his eyes, the same look he had given her when they first met.

He didn't speak to her immediately, leaving her in suspense. Instead, he turned to address the entire group. *"You have all proven yourselves exceptional—far more than mere travellers of time. And now, a new adventure awaits."*

Ajay, always the first to dive into the details, leaned forward eagerly. *"What is it this time? Where are we going?"*

Revanth's eyes twinkled with mystery. *"Let's just say... it will be unlike anything you've ever experienced. This time, deeper forces are at play, and the path ahead is intertwined with stories older than time itself."*

Vishwa grinned widely. *"Is it going to be dangerous?"*

Revanth laughed, his voice echoing with a sense of adventure. "*Dangerous? Perhaps. Thrilling? Absolutely.*" he added, turning back to Siya, "*I have an inkling now why we were drawn together. But to discover the truth… you'll have to take the next step with me*"

Siya's heart raced. "*Me? Why?*"

Revanth grinned, enigmatic as ever. "*All in good time. Some answers you must discover for yourself.*"

Before they could say anything else, the air shimmered again, and a new portal formed, swirling with vibrant colours, ancient and alive

"*Are you ready for the next adventure?*" Revanth asked, his eyes alight with mystery and excitement.

The children nodded eagerly, unable to contain their anticipation. Meanwhile, Siya's mind raced with unspoken questions—especially about Revanth's mysterious connection to her—his words still echoing in her thoughts.

With one last glance at the softly glowing conch in her hand, Siya stepped forward with the others—ready to follow Revanth once more into the unknown.

Together, they stepped into the portal, leaving the familiar world behind—ready to write the next chapter of their extraordinary story.

The Harmony Six will return!